D0734850

NO EXIT FROM BROOKLYN

No Exit

A NICK

From

DELVECCHIO

Brooklyn

MYSTERY

Robert J. Randisi

St. Martin's Press
New York

241600

Design by John Fontana

Library of Congress Cataloging in Publication Data

Randisi, Robert J.
    No exit from Brooklyn.

    "A Thomas Dunne book."
    I. Title.
PS3568.A53N6   1987   813'.54   87-4472
ISBN 0-312-00169-X

First Edition
10 9 8 7 6 5 4 3 2 1

For Anna, Christopher, and Matthew
and
for the denizens of Brooklyn

NO EXIT FROM BROOKLYN

PROLOGUE

T he whole thing started—
Let me rephrase that: The *entire* thing started because of boredom and a middle-of-the-night phone call. It sure wasn't because I needed the money. My bank account was pretty healthy at the time, as a matter of fact. I'd just finished a case that would keep me in groceries, rent, and fast food for months, and that was all I ever really needed.

But if there's one thing I hate, it's being bored.

I went into this business of private investigation after an incident that got me pensioned off the police department with one-third of my salary instead of a prison sentence, and I had to find something that would allow me to do the things I was

1

good at. The same "rabbi" who saved me from being railroaded off the job and into prison got me my P.I.'s license, and that was four years ago. Since that time I'd taken a lot of cases in the name of boredom that I shouldn't have, and you'd think I would have learned from that.

Not a chance.

When I get bored, I make the same mistakes all over again.

So the first connection I had with the entire affair was a middle-of-the-night phone call—which I hate almost as much as being bored.

I didn't know how many times the goddamn phone had rung already when I knocked it off its perch and groped about the floor for it.

"Hum, yeah, wha—"

"This Delvecchio?" a man's voice asked.

"Mmm hmm."

"You the private eye?" he asked. I didn't recognize his voice, but then in the middle of the night I probably wouldn't recognize my own father's voice.

"Is this an obscene phone call?"

"Forget the whole thing, pal."

"Fine by me, *pal*."

"No, I mean it, Delvecchio," the guy said. "Forget the whole thing. Got it?"

He stretched out the two words when he said "whole thing," like it really meant something.

"Look, pal," I said, swinging my feet around to the floor, "you woke me up in the middle of the night to tell me to forget the whole thing? Shit, I'd rather get an obscene phone call. At least they make sense."

"Delvecchio, you better wake up and listen to what I'm telling you. If you want to stay healthy, just forget the whole thing."

2

"Hey," I said amiably, "it's forgotten—" but he had hung up with a loud click.

It was so dark that I couldn't see the phone in my hand, but I knew it was there so I stared at it for a few seconds, then said, "Screw it," left it off the hook, got back under the covers, and went back to sleep.

1
___

I wasn't really *in* my office the next day, but the same phone line in my one-room office also goes into the adjoining three-room apartment. Summer was knocking on the door, and I was caught trying to decide whether to be bored with the T.V., a book, or going down the block to OTB, so I welcomed the interruption.

I answered on the second ring, so real was my dread of boredom.

"Delvecchio."

"Are you the private detective?"

"I'm *a* private detective."

The voice was a girl's, and she didn't sound real sure of

herself, so I let my remarks end there and waited. It was up to her to decide if I was *the* private detective she wanted.

"I—I'd like to hire you, but I don't want to come to your office."

"Make a suggestion."

"Can we meet somewhere?"

"Sure. Near you or near me?"

"I live in Bay Ridge, but I don't want to meet there."

"All right. Do you know where the Promenade is?"

"Sure."

"When would you like to meet?"

"In an hour?"

"That's fine with me. Can you tell me your name?"

"Jodi," she said. "I'll meet you in an hour."

She hung up before we could arrange some way for one of us to recognize the other.

Well, at least I had boredom beat for a while.

The official name for it was the Esplanade, but everyone in Brooklyn called it the Promenade. I don't know why, they—we—just do. It's sort of a park without grass that hangs over the Brooklyn-Queens Expressway, and from it Brooklynites and tourists alike can stare out across the East River at the classic skyline of New York City. It was a nice mile walk from my office on Sackett Street.

Of course, it wouldn't be complete without Jake and his hot-dog stand.

That was where I saw Jodi Hayworth for the first time, standing by Jake's stand with a handful of hot dog smothered in onions.

I walked over to where she was standing, a girl who was probably about nineteen or twenty with long, straight blonde hair, incredible blue cat's eyes on a tomboy face, and an attitude and demeanor that said, "You can feel the cushions,

5

buster, but you can't sit down." Coincidentally, she reminded me of another Jody—Jodie Foster, the way she looked in a movie called *Carny*. Tomboyish, but sexy as hell.

She was wearing jeans and a tank top, and she didn't have an ounce of excess flesh on her. She had taut breasts, a nonexistent waist, and long, trim legs. On her feet were a pair of calf-high boots with heels that added a couple of inches to her height, which in bare feet I would have put at five-four.

I spotted her because it wasn't noon yet, so the office workers were still at their desks and not having lunch on the Promenade. There was a couple standing at the rail, another sitting on a bench, an elderly woman walking a dog, and this girl. It was either the woman with the dog or the girl.

I opted for the girl.

"Jodi?"

"Are you Nick Delvecchio?" she asked, turning her attention from the hot dog to me.

"That's me."

I looked at the hot dog in her hand and saw that beneath the onions there was no mustard.

"I think I love you," I said.

Her eyes widened and she said, "What?" as if she wasn't sure she heard me right.

"The hot dog," I said, pointing. "No mustard, right?"

"I hate mustard!" she said, with feeling. "I wouldn't put it on my worst enemy."

"I thought I was the only person in the world that felt that way," I said. "This must be love."

"Please," she said, as if she suddenly thought I was running a line.

I don't know. Maybe I was.

"Build me one, will you, Jake?"

"Onions, no mustard," Jake said, shaking his head. "Yer both nuts."

6

If anyone ever asked me what Brooklyn was, I'd tell them to go and talk to Jake. He was Brooklyn born and bred, ran his little hot-dog stand nine months out of the year, and spent the other three months in his condo in Florida. He was built like a fire hydrant, his seamed face defying you to guess his age. His fingers were almost like sausages themselves, but they were deft as they plucked hot dogs from the water, laid them gently on the bun, and then built it to your specifications. Sometimes I'm almost tempted to order one with everything just to watch his hands fly around.

He handed me mine and I paid him for both.

"Let's go over by the rail," I said. I led the way to the rail, from which we could see the World Trade Center's twin towers. We could hear the traffic whooshing by on the Brooklyn-Queens Expressway beneath us.

"Okay," I said, "I'm Delvecchio, you're Jodi. What can I do for you?"

"I've got a problem I'd like to talk to you about."

"Well, sit down and talk, then."

We sat on a bench, still facing the city. The breeze coming off the water was cool, and strong enough to whip her fine hair about her face. She was carrying a large shoulder bag, and she brought it around so that she could sit with it at her feet. Close up, her eyes were even more startling.

"Why don't we start with your full name."

"It's Hayworth, Jodi Hayworth."

"All right, Miss Hayworth. Why don't you tell me what your problem is."

"Uh, well, I want you to find something for me."

"Something that you lost," I asked, "or something that was taken from you?"

"It's something that's missing—actually, it *is* something that was stolen . . . from my house."

It was obvious that she didn't have her story straight yet.

7

Oh, she knew what her problem was, all right, but she just wasn't sure how much she wanted to tell me.

I decided to let her go on for a while and see what developed.

"What is it?" I asked, taking a huge bite out of my hot dog.

She made a face and said, "It's what my mother calls an 'object of art,' or something. It's kind of, uh, round with a little, um, hole in the middle—well, actually it's more of a big hole—really, it's more like all hole—ah, shit," she cursed shortly. "I kind of have my own name for the thing."

"Which is?"

"I call it 'the hole thing.'"

"The *hole* thing?" I asked, my late-night call coming back to me in a rush. He hadn't said forget the *whole* thing, he'd said forget the *hole* thing!

Suddenly, I wasn't bored at all anymore.

2

"All right, Miss Hayworth," I said, "where was this 'hole thing' stolen from?"

"I told you, my home."

"Oh, that's right, you did tell me that," I said, shaking my head. "Where do you live?"

"In Bay Ridge. I told you that on the phone."

"With your parents?"

She made a little face before answering, "Yeah."

"Was the house burglarized?"

"Huh? Oh, yeah, the house was robbed."

"What was taken?"

"Oh, just the hole thing," she answered with a shrug. She

held her hands apart in an attempt to indicate the size of the item we were discussing. There was still a little less than half a hot dog in her right hand.

"Was it like a statue?"

"Yeah, it's a round thing set on a base. It's kind of a dull gray in color." It was difficult for her to use her hands while holding the hot dog, so she stuffed what was left into her mouth, where it sat half in and half out. As she used her hands it appeared that the thing was about a foot or so high.

"And nothing else was taken?"

"No," she said around the hot dog, then bit and chewed, holding the final small chunk in her hand.

She crossed her legs nervously, and I imagined I could see her leg muscles moving through the tight jeans.

"What did the police say?"

"I, uh, didn't call the police," she said, avoiding my eyes.

"What about your parents?"

"They're . . . away," she admitted, and the picture started to get a little clearer.

"Your parents are away, someone broke into the house and stole this 'hole' statue, and you didn't call the police. Have I got that right?"

"That's right."

"And nothing else was stolen?"

"That's right," she said again, choosing that moment to examine the remainder of her hot dog.

I put my hands in my lap and regarded her tomboy face in profile for a few moments. I've always hated girls with small noses, but this one was all right.

It was too bad she was a liar.

Well, maybe "liar" was too harsh a word, but at the very least she was feeding me a line of bullshit I was finding hard to digest.

"Miss Hayworth, if you really want to hire me, you're going to have to tell me the truth."

10

"What—"

"Don't give me that surprised look, young lady, and don't try and con me with that little-girl face. I've been conned by experts."

She lifted one corner of her mouth in the kind of gesture kids use when they realize they're not going to get what they want.

"Come on, Jodi," I said, taking a stab in the dark, "what'd you do, hock the thing?"

Her head jerked up, and she looked at me in obvious surprise.

"How did you—"

"It was just a guess, but I'm generally a good guesser," I said. "Why don't you tell me the truth, now?"

"That is the truth," she said, toying with the strap on her tote bag. "I needed some money, so I hocked the thing."

"Where?"

"Pawnshop on Atlantic Avenue."

"Go on."

"Well, I told the guy I'd be back to claim the damned thing in a couple of days . . ." she said, trailing off sadly.

"And he sold it out from under you?"

"Yeah, the creep. Said he got too good an offer for it to turn it down."

"How much is the thing worth, Jodi?"

She shrugged and said, "Shit, I don't know."

"How much did you get for it?"

"Two fifty."

"Two hundred and fifty dollars?"

She nodded.

"Do you know what *he* got for it?"

She shrugged.

"Bastard wouldn't tell me. He wouldn't even tell me who he sold it to so I could try to buy it back."

I decided not to ask her where she had gotten the money to try and buy it back. I figured she'd lie again.

"What's going to happen when your parents get back and find it gone?"

She expelled her breath in a disgusted rush and said, "Diane'll have a shit fit."

"Diane?"

"My mother," she said, distaste obvious in her tone.

"And your father?"

"Damn it," she said, "none of this would have happened if—"

"If what?"

"If I didn't need the money," she said, but I had a feeling that hadn't been what she was going to say before.

"When are your parents coming back?"

"That's another problem. They weren't supposed to be back until next month, but I got a telegram saying they're coming back next week."

"You're really in a bind, huh?"

"What do you think?" She turned and looked at me, giving me the full benefit of those blue eyes. "Look, Mr. Delvecchio, couldn't you please try and find it for me? I'll buy it back from whoever bought it."

"Do you have the money?"

"I do now—and I have enough to pay you, if that's what you're worried about," she added. She leaned over to start rummaging about in her bag, but I stopped her.

"Don't worry about my fee, okay?"

She looked up at me from her bent-over position and said, "Then you'll help me?"

"Sure," I said, thinking about boredom, a middle-of-the-night call, and a tomboy face with big cat's eyes.

"Sure," I said again, "why not?"

I found out later why not, but later is always too late.

*   *   *

I asked her where the hockshop was on Atlantic Avenue, and
she said she didn't remember the cross streets but she could
drive me there. I told her I wanted to go back to my office first
so she could sign a contract. She asked if that was necessary,
and I said that it was with me. For my own reasons I try to
keep my business as up-and-up as possible.

"Where's your car?" I asked.

"Down the block."

"Lead on."

She took the lead and I admired the way her jeans clung to
her firm behind. Her waist made me think of those T.V. com-
mercials about not being able to pinch an inch. On the way out
she tossed the rest of her hot dog into a trash barrel.

The car was a black sporty job with no top. Normally you've
got to have a lot of balls to park a car like that in downtown
Brooklyn, but she'd gotten away with it. There wasn't so much
as a cigarette lighter or hubcap missing.

After she'd signed one of my contracts for me, we walked
down from the third floor where I lived and worked. I'd forgone
a retainer for now, at least until I made sure I could do something for her.

The house where I lived and worked was a converted
brownstone on Sackett Street, spitting distance from the
Brooklyn Bridge if you're a good spitter, and it stood four stories high. The neighborhood was pretty shitty and nothing like
where Jodi lived in Bay Ridge, which, along with Canarsie and
Marine Park, was one of the last havens of Brooklyn.

"I like it down here," Jodi said as we walked down the front
steps.

"You're crazy."

"Don't you?"

"Sure, but I *know* I'm crazy."

Also, it was good for my business, such as it was. Court

13

Street wasn't very far away, where most of the Brooklyn lawyers had their offices. All of the court buildings were nearby as well, on Adams, Livingston, Schermerhorn, and other streets. Both bridges to—or from—Manhattan were close by, and there were plenty of fast-food places on Fulton Street and in the Albee Mall. This area, Brooklyn Heights, is one of the busiest in all of Brooklyn. My office/apartment sits right on the boundary between the Heights and Red Hook.

Brooklyn has been bad-mouthed in a lot of places. "Only the dead know Brooklyn," Thomas Wolfe said—but I live here, too, so don't say it around me.

She went around to the driver's side, and I hopped over the door on the passenger's side.

"Why'd you hock it?" I asked after she'd gotten us rolling.

She removed a strand of her fine hair that had blown into her mouth and said, "I needed the money."

"For what?"

"Is that important, or are you just nosy?"

"I guess I'm just nosy," I admitted. "If it becomes important, I'll ask you again."

"Okay."

"And you'll answer."

She hesitated, then said, "Okay," with a short nod.

She made a couple of turns, and I was about to tell her that she was headed away from our destination when she said in an exasperated tone, "Where the hell is Atlantic Avenue?"

I laughed and directed her to the Flatbush Avenue Extension. We were traveling south, toward Grand Army Plaza, and I asked her, "Which side of the extension is it on?"

She thought a moment, then said, "I think we have to turn right."

"Okay, we'll try it," I said. "If it's not there, we'll go the other way."

She drove with confidence, but she wasn't a good driver.

14

She seemed to be the kind who felt the road belonged to her and everyone else better get out of the way.

As she approached the place where Flatbush, Atlantic, and Fourth Avenue all come together—a corner where you can get almost anything, from chicken to chicks to a Long Island Railroad train—I said, "Hang a right, Jodi."

She did so, and I added, "Keep your eyes open."

We were halfway between Flatbush and the Brooklyn-Queens Expressway when she cried out, "There it is," and pointed across the street.

"Pull over."

There were no available spots, so she pulled in by a hydrant, in front of a Syrian restaurant.

"There," she said again, pointing.

I saw the place she meant. It was a dingy little hole-in-the-wall that I'd never noticed before, but then hockshops were not among my regular hangouts. There was a sign over the door that said "Antiques, bought and sold."

"Jodi, is this thing valuable?" I asked. "I mean, would this guy know what he was getting?"

"I don't know. He didn't act like it was anything so great. It's just this ugly little, uh, round—"

"Yeah, I know," I interrupted her, "hole thing."

"Right."

"Okay, you wait for me here."

"Can't I come in?"

"I don't want the guy to see you," I said. "When were you in?"

"Uh, last week the first time, and then again a couple of days ago."

"Did you give him a hard time the second time?"

"Oh yeah. I screamed at him, the creep."

15

"Then let's assume that he'd remember you."

"Hell, yes."

"Okay," I said, hopping out of the car, "wait right here."

"Gonna threaten him?"

"I'm gonna con him," I said, and crossed the street when there was a lull in the traffic.

3

The hockshop stood on Atlantic Avenue, just off of Smith Street, situated between a laundromat and a junk store. In fact, most of the stores along Atlantic Avenue could be described as junk stores—but then one man's junk is another man's treasure, I guess.

Most of the stores on these blocks were either antique shops or restaurants, but no Burger Kings for Atlantic Avenue, no sir. There were Syrian restaurants, Greek restaurants, pizza places, one legit Italian restaurant, all of this in the ten-block expanse that ran from BQE to Flatbush Avenue. The surprising thing about this stretch is that there were very few bars. There were plenty of those a few blocks over, on Schermerhorn Street and Livingston Street.

When I opened the door to the place, I thought it was going to fall off its hinges, but it held. A small bell over the door announced my arrival.

The place had a thick, musty smell, and it was cluttered with all kinds of stuff hanging from the walls.

"Can I help you?" a voice asked.

I peered around and finally located the source of the voice. He was standing behind a wire-mesh screen. Shit, I thought, this place is right out of *The Pawnbroker*.

"Are you the proprietor?"

"Yes, I'm Mr. Wallach. Can I help you?"

Through the screen I could see a portly, gray-haired man of about fifty-five or so. His hands were dirty, and he had a couple of fingertip smudges on his broad forehead.

I took out one of my business cards and handed it to him beneath the mesh.

"A private detective?" he asked, reading the card. "What do you want to do, Mr. Private Eye, hock your gun?" he then asked, laughing.

"Gun?" I asked. "No, Mr. Wallach, you've got the wrong fella. I don't carry a gun. They scare me."

He looked disappointed and put my card down on the counter.

"What do you want, then?" He had a slight Jewish accent.

"I deal in art objects, Mr. Wallach," I told him. "I'm hired to track down lost and missing ones, that is. A client of mine had one stolen a few weeks ago, and I'm given to understand that it was in your shop as recently as last week."

"I don't deal in stolen goods, mister!" he told me with forced indignation. "*You* got the wrong man."

"Calm down, Mr. Wallach, calm down," I said. "I'm not accusing you of anything, believe me. I'm sure that if the ob-

18

ject I'm looking for was indeed in your shop, you came by it quite innocently."

"You can bet I'm innocent," he said, but I would never have taken him up on such a bet.

"I'm also sure you had no idea of the item's true value."

His ears perked up and he craned his neck as he repeated, "True value? What do you mean, true value?"

"The piece I'm talking about is worth quite a lot of money, Mr. Wallach, which is why my client has authorized me to pay a ten percent finder's fee to anyone who can help me locate it."

"Finder's fee?" he asked. "Ten percent? What would that come to?"

"Well, if it's genuine, I suppose ten percent would amount to, oh, five, maybe six thousand dollars. It could even be more."

"Six thousand dollars?" he squeaked. "What kind of item could I have in my shop worth that much?" he asked, looking around at his goods.

"Well, I'll describe the item to you, Mr. Wallach. It was about so high," I said, moving my hands, "and it was round, with a big hole, and it was set on a base—"

"That thing?" he exclaimed, slapping both hands to his face. "That thing?"

"Then you have it."

"Oh, my—I had such a thing only two days ago. It was brought here last week by a blonde girl—"

"A blonde girl, you say?" I asked. "With pretty blue eyes, a pointed nose . . ."

"That's her. She brought it to me last week, and I bought it from her for two hundred and fifty dollars."

"Two fifty!" I said, looking amazed. "That was quite a bargain, Mr. Wallach. Still, to give her that much, you must have had some idea of its worth."

19

"I knew it was an art object, and I have some customers who are interested in such things."

"Well, if you can show me where it is, I'm sure I could offer you a little more than ten percent—"

"Oy," he said, covering his face with his hands, leaving more fingertip smudges.

"You do have it, don't you?"

"I had it, I had it!" he cried into his hands.

"You sold it?" I asked, trying to sound disappointed.

He nodded.

"All right, Mr. Wallach, let's not get excited about this. I'm sure we can work something out."

"We could?" he asked, opening his hands and peeking out.

"Sure, Mr.—ah, what's your first name?"

"Sid, Sid is my first name," he said, eager to please.

"Well, all right, Sid. I'm sure you have a record of who you sold it to, don't you?"

He stared at me for a moment, and then his face lit up.

"I have it, yes." Suddenly, though, his face took on a shrewd, crafty look, and I knew the time had come. "I really couldn't give it to you, however," he said. "My records are confidential."

"I realize that, Sid, I really do," I said carefully, "and I would never ask you to compromise yourself, but I'm sure that if we can recover the item, I could get my client to go for more than ten percent. Perhaps even, uh, ten thousand dollars?"

It was a ridiculous figure, but his greed overcame his common sense.

"Ten thousand?"

"That is, unless you can afford to buy the item back yourself. I'm sure the person who bought it knows what they have."

His face fell, and he said, "I—I couldn't afford to buy it back—"

"Ten thousand is still a nice profit from a two-hundred-and-fifty-dollar layout."

"Wait," he told me, holding his hands out, "wait, wait, don't go away."

He disappeared into a back room, and I could hear him rummaging around, talking to himself. Finally he returned with a small, orange card in his hand.

"I have it!" he cried triumphantly. "I have it!"

"Excellent," I said. "Could I see it, please?"

"Of course, of course," he said, pushing it at me from beneath the mesh.

It was neatly typed on a typewriter that was missing a "v" and about to lose a "u," but it was legible.

"Can I take this, Sid?"

"Take it, take it. It has my name and phone number on the back."

"Indeed it does." I tucked the card away in my pocket and said, "Well, Sid, this may be it. I'll check this out, and if we recover the item, you will be quite a few dollars richer."

When I left, the old man looked decidedly hopeful.

"Did you get it?"

"I got it," I said, showing her the orange card.

She screamed and threw her arms around me, saying, "You're wonderful."

My mouth was pressed against her bare shoulder and her breasts were pressed against my chest as she showed her appreciation. The flesh of her shoulder was smooth and slightly damp from perspiration, and her hair had that fragrance that only blonde hair does. I started to respond the way a man normally will when a vibrant, healthy young girl throws herself into his lap.

And she noticed.

"Thank you, Nick," she said, staring into my face with her arms around my neck. For a moment her mouth was invitingly close, but before I could decide to take advantage, she was back on her side of the car, behind the wheel.

"Just to show you how much I appreciate this," she said, "I'm going to take you to an early dinner."

"And pay my fee, I hope."

She laughed and said, "That, too."

I checked my watch and it was getting kind of late in the day.

"I guess we can check this address out tomorrow."

"Sure," she agreed. "Getting it was the important part, and I sure hired the right man for that job."

I directed her to a little restaurant I liked on Pacific Street, where it wouldn't matter how we were dressed. We drove there and celebrated over some good Italian food and a couple of bottles of red wine, and by the time I knew it we were in my apartment and my hands were roaming around beneath her tank top. . . .

The next thing I knew it was morning and I was staring at the ceiling above my bed. I didn't have a hangover exactly, but there was a buzzing in my ears, and my tongue had somehow turned into Velcro. My arms were spread straight out to the side so that it didn't take a genius to figure out that I was alone in bed. Jodi was gone who knew how long.

After about ten years I got myself up into a seated position with my feet on the floor. My clothes were strewn about the floor, and there was a dead soldier lying against one wall. I tried to remember how many such bottles we had emptied, but all I could remember was that I seemed to be doing most of the drinking.

That's right, I thought, I did most of the drinking, and who was it kept filling my glass?

22

No, I thought, don't tell me. She couldn't have been that kind of girl. . . .

I staggered out of bed and retrieved my pants from the floor. My wallet was still in my pocket, and I quickly went through it with a feeling of dread that proved unwarranted. I felt like a heel when I discovered that my cash was still there.

I rubbed my eyes and dropped my arms to my sides, mentally apologizing to Jodi. Maybe a shower would bring me back to life.

I started picking up my clothes, and when I reached my jacket, I remembered that all-important orange card, the reason for the previous night's celebration.

I reached into my jacket pocket and didn't find it. I checked another pocket with the same results. I searched all my pockets and then checked them again and still came up empty. I went through my apartment, my office, and my wallet.

The card was gone, with Jodi.

I didn't see her again for two weeks.

4

The cops found me in the corner laundromat.

Mrs. Goldstein was regaling me with the latest neighborhood gossip when they walked in. They were both in plain clothes, but everything about them said "cop."

Mrs. Goldstein is sort of the neighborhood snoop, for want of a better word. She's a lovable Jewish widow who, since the death of her beloved Abe five years earlier, had sort of taken all of us under her wing. She kept track of the comings and goings in the area, dispensed kindly, well-meant, frequently useless advice, and was always trying to fix me up with one of her nieces.

She's a nice lady, and I like her.

24

The laundromat doubled as the neighborhood social club. When you're a bachelor and you do your own laundry, you tend to keep meeting the same people around the washers and driers. There was Mr. Quinn, the Greek grocer whose wife never did laundry; there was "Mad Dog" Bolinsky, a huge sanitation worker who lived alone and didn't really like anyone but cats and kids; and there was my neighbor across the hall, the lovely and talented Kit Karson. Well, actually her name was Samantha Karson, but she wrote romance novels under the name Kit. When I asked why she would change her name from something as pretty as Samantha to something as terse as Kit, she said she was saving her real name for her important work. Sam thought that as a private eye, I would sooner or later be the source for that work.

Anyway, I was taking my shorts out of the dryer, listening to Mrs. Goldstein tell me about Mrs. Munchik's boy, the one who couldn't keep a job because of his drinking and womanizing, when the cops walked in and spotted me. Even if they hadn't had "cop" written all over them, I'd have known them for what they were, because I knew one of them by sight. His name was Detective Matucci, and we had managed to go through the academy together without a civil word passing between us.

"All right, scumbag," he said, approaching me, "let's go."

"What kind of way is that for a young man to talk?" Mrs. Goldstein asked him immediately.

"Who's this," Matucci asked, "your mother?"

"God forbid I was *your* mother, young man," Mrs. Goldstein replied before I could, "I'd teach you how to talk to decent people."

"Oh, he's got an excuse, Mrs. Goldstein," I explained. "You see, this man is a policeman. He's allowed to talk to people like that, aren't you, Vito?"

"Aye," Matucci said to me, waggling the forefinger of his

right hand in my face, "you don't call me by my first name, shitface."

"This is a policeman?" Mrs. Goldstein asked, incredulously.

"That he is, Mrs. Goldstein. One of New York's finest." I would have said "one of New York's finest assholes," but I didn't want to redirect Mrs. Goldstein's ire at that moment. I was enjoying seeing it aimed at Vito Matucci.

Matucci was short for a cop, to his everlasting shame. His father and uncles and brothers were all officers, and all six-footers, while "Little Vito" was barely five-seven. He tried to make up for it with a hard nose and a big mouth, and if his size had been all he had to overcome, he might have made it. Unfortunately for Vito, he was a complete asshole, no matter how you looked at him.

"Who's your friend?" I asked.

"Detective Weinstock," the man said, which immediately put him high on Mrs. Goldstein's list.

"Do you know Moshe Weinstock, from Canarsie?" she asked him.

"I'm sorry, ma'am, no, I don't."

"Polite," she said, smiling triumphantly at Matucci. "You could learn something from your friend."

"They're not friends," I corrected her, "they're partners," and from the look on Weinstock's face I could see I'd hit the nail right on the head.

When you're a complete asshole like Matucci, it's hard to hide it from anyone, least of all your partner.

"Could you come with us please, Mr. Delvecchio?" Weinstock said. "Our boss would like to talk to you."

"How'd you know where to find me?"

"The bitch across the hall told us where you were," Matucci said, further shocking poor Mrs. Goldstein.

26

I'd have to remember to thank Sam. I'd tell her what Matucci called her. She'd find it interesting.

"Where you boys working out of these days?"

"You don't have to tell him nothing," Matucci said, balling his hands up into fists. I knew he wouldn't swing at me, because the last time he did, I broke his nose for him. "Let's go, Delvecchio."

"Let me get finished with my shorts," I said, transferring the pair in my right hand to my left and reaching into the dryer for the rest.

"Forget about your shorts," Matucci said. "We're leaving—now!"

"Right now?"

"Now."

"Have it your way."

As we headed for the door, Mrs. Goldstein called out, "I'll take care of your laundry, Nicky."

She would, too—all except for the pair of shorts I'd stuffed into my back pocket.

I was grateful for the fact that Matucci drove to the Seventy-eighth Precinct, on Bergen Street. The few times we had ridden in a radio car together, I had discovered that he was such a notoriously poor driver that he couldn't operate the car and talk at the same time. I don't know what Weinstock's excuse was, but he didn't speak either.

When we pulled up in front of the precinct and Matucci had turned off the motor, he turned on his mouth again.

"Okay, skell, out."

"Skell" was a word you learned when you joined the police department. I don't know exactly who coined it, but it generally meant that muck you find "at the bottom of the barrel."

"You still have a way with words, Vito."

27

"Look, mother—"

"Let's go upstairs, Matucci," Weinstock suggested. "The sooner we turn him over to the boss, the sooner we can be rid of him."

"You've got a point there, Weinstock," Matucci said. "Let's go."

They took me upstairs to the second floor where the squad room was located. The walls of the run-down building were a kind of sickly lime green, complemented by peeling paint and cracks in the wall. In other words, it hadn't changed since I had been a patrolman there.

"Sit down," Weinstock said. "I'll tell the lieutenant you're here."

"Thanks."

Matucci scowled and walked away while Weinstock went into the lieutenant's office. I wondered who was in charge of the squad these days.

"Mr. Delvecchio," Weinstock called. He was waving me over, standing half in and half out of the lieutenant's office.

I got up and walked to the office, with Matucci suddenly behind me. Weinstock stood aside to allow me to enter and Matucci pushed his way between us. Weinstock gave the back of his partner's head an annoyed look.

"This is Lieutenant Wager," Weinstock said, but there was no introduction necessary. Wager and I knew each other.

He was a big, beefy man with red cheeks, and during his years as a desk officer he had been notorious for sending radio cars to restaurants to pick up his complimentary meals—sometimes three or four a tour. From his girth, he looked as if he still did.

I had heard a story once when I first came on the job from an old-timer who had gotten tired of being Wager's gopher. Seems that when he and his partner were sent for coffee, he'd stopped the radio car by an alley, gotten out, pissed in the coffee, and then delivered it to Wager. He didn't know if Wager had drunk it, but that had been the last time he and his partner had made a coffee run for the lieutenant.

"Lieutenant Wager," I said. Although he was in a new position of authority, I was oddly gratified to find that he had not risen in rank.

"Delvecchio and I know each other, Weinstock," Wager said. "You can go and close the door on your way out."

"Yes, sir."

"Sit down, Delvecchio."

I turned to pull a chair over, and Wager suddenly said, "What the hell is that?"

Weinstock and Matucci stopped short, and I turned to look at Wager.

"That," Wager said, pointing behind me.

I reached behind me and pulled the shorts from my pocket. Most of my shorts are solid color, but these had been a gift from an old girlfriend at Valentine's Day, white with red hearts with an arrow through them.

"These are my shorts."

"What the hell are they doing here?"

"When your torrid twosome came for me, I was at the laundromat doing my laundry. They wouldn't let me finish."

Wager threw Matucci a dirty look, as if he knew the asshole was to blame.

"Look, he's just—"

"Shut up and get out, Matucci!"

Matucci's face suffused with blood. He threw me a murderous glare, and then slunk from the room. Weinstock followed, and shut the door behind him.

"Get those things out of sight and sit down!" Wager snapped at me.

I balled them up and tucked them deeper in my back pocket, where they made an uncomfortable bulge.

"You know," I said, taking a seat, "if you wanted to talk over old times, you didn't have to send two of your best to get me. An engraved invitation would have done."

"Shut up," Wager said. "I didn't have you brought here to listen to your lip. I had enough of that when you were a cop here."

"Sure, Lieutenant."

"You know a man named Sid Wallach?"

"Never heard of him."

"That's funny," Wager said. "This was found in his pocket last night."

He held something out to me, and I recognized it as one of my business cards.

"So? I give those things out all the time. I have no control over who ends up with them."

"I see."

"Who was this guy, anyway?" I asked. "Somebody you threw into a drunk tank?"

"No," Wager said, tossing the card on his desk. "Sid Wallach owned a pawnshop on Atlantic Avenue."

"A pawnshop?"

"Does that ring a bell?"

"Actually, it does," I said, thinking of Jodi Hayworth for the first time in a week.

"Care to tell me what?" Wager asked, lacing his fat fingers on the desk top.

"I don't know," I said. "Care to tell me why you're asking?"

"Mr. Sid Wallach was found in his shop last night," Wager said, watching my face carefully.

"Found?"

"Dead."

"Dead?" I repeated.

"And tortured—and he had your business card in his pocket," Wager reminded me. He crossed his pudgy arms across his chest and announced imperiously, "I'm waiting for an explanation."

30

5

W ager's problem had always been that he expected
people to bow to his rank. He never realized that
people respect a man, not a rank. Now, sitting with his arms
folded, he seemed to think I would fall apart because he was
confronting me with a business card.

Well, I didn't, but I think I surprised the shit out of him.
I cooperated.

I run my business by the book as much as I can—which
was why I had Jodi Hayworth sign a contract—and it was men
like Wager who were the reason. He would have liked nothing
better than to have me hold out on him so he could pull my
license.

I didn't give him the chance.

I told him exactly what I had been hired to do a week ago by Jodi Hayworth, and I ran it down for him by the numbers, holding nothing back. There was nothing that it would have done me any good *to* hold back, so I didn't mind opening up for him.

"Is that everything?" he asked when I stopped talking.

"That's all I've got, Wager," I said, and he looked downright disappointed.

"You never went back to that hockshop after that?"

"For what reason?"

"And you never saw the girl again?"

"I never even got paid, Wager."

That seemed to cheer him up some, so I didn't bother telling him that I had settled for another form of compensation.

"If you've been straight with me, Delvecchio, you've got nothing to worry about, but if I find out that you held out—"

"I like my license, Lieutenant," I said, cutting him off. "I'm not holding out."

"I'm sure you like your license," Wager said, "considering how you got it."

I let the remark go, because he was trying to get my goat.

"Can I go now?"

"Be my guest. Don't think I want to see you any longer than I have to."

"I enjoyed it, too, Lieutenant," I said, standing up. "What are the chances of getting a ride home?"

"What do you think?" he replied, scowling.

"That's okay, I'll get one downstairs."

As I left his office, he was reaching for the phone. I knew he was going to call downstairs to the big front desk—what a friend of mine used to call the B.F.D.—and let them know that nobody was to give me a ride home. Actually, I could have just walked home, but it would do my heart good to get a ride from one of the radio cars.

I went downstairs to see if I had any friends left in the precinct where I had once worked.

I had been a cop in the seven-eight for three years when an incident occurred which changed my outlook on life—and, eventually, my career.

Up to that point I had been a pretty easygoing guy, but I tried to break up a fight one day and suddenly found myself on the receiving end of a beating from *both* parties. It had been a fairly severe pounding, since they had gotten ahold of my nightstick and used it on me. It could have been worse, they told me in the hospital. They could have gotten my gun.

Four months later I was back on the job with a new outlook. Never again would I take a beating like that from *anyone*, no matter what the situation. They told us in the academy that force was to be met by equal force and never by *more* than equal force. In other words, you couldn't use your gun unless the perp had a gun.

Bullshit.

From that point on in my life I used as much force as I needed to use to keep myself in one piece. Never again would I lie in a hospital bed wondering if I'd ever walk or scratch my nose—or fuck—again.

Over the next two years I went before three Internal Affairs Review Boards for excessive violence, and was threatened with three more. I couldn't help it. As soon as I felt I was in danger, I lashed out. I took a couple of suspensions from I.A.D. rulings, but nothing real heavy—until that last time.

I overreacted in that last situation, and I hurt the guy pretty severely. Not as badly as *I* had been hurt, but he went to the hospital. When they called me onto the carpet, they told me I

33

had really fucked up this time. The kid's father was a politician—an upwardly mobile politician—and he wanted my balls.

My only ace was that the kid—who was eighteen, six-three, two hundred pounds—was breaking the law at the time the incident occurred. In fact, he was robbing an old woman and was armed with homemade blackjack. When he turned on me with it, I could have shot him, but I used my nightstick instead. I broke his arm and opened his head for him, and that was that.

Until I.A.D. reared its ugly head with the news that his politician father wanted my ass—and they were going to give it to him.

Or so they thought.

You see, after they gave him my hide, they were going to let him take his "little boy" home—only I wasn't ready to go along with that. I threatened to break the story to the papers, so a compromise had to be made.

I came out of it with a one-third disability pension and a P.I. license.

The politician came out of it with his little boy.

It was now four years later, and I still had my pension and an office on Sackett Street.

All the politician had was a grave, because his son was shot dead six months later by a cop during an attempted armed robbery.

First chance they got, they'd yank my ticket, only I'd never give them the chance. Not even if my business card was found in a dead man's pocket.

"Hey, Nicky D.!"

I turned and saw Police Officer Neal Citrola bearing down on me. Neal and I had come on the job together.

"Hi, Neal."

"How are you doing, boy?" Neal asked, slapping me on the back.

"Fine, Neal, fine. You coming or going?"

"Just coming on, man. Why?"

"I need a ride."

"Where?"

"Home."

"No sweat. I'll get my unit and take you, right after roll call."

"Uh, I should tell you that Wager called down . . ."

"You talked to Wager? That asshole!"

"Yeah. I'm sure he called down and left word that I wasn't to be given a ride."

"Well shit, I'll just grab an extra unit and take you right now."

"I don't want to get you into trouble, Neal."

"No trouble, Nicky. I'll just tell the desk sergeant that I'm picking up a sandwich for Wager and I need a car."

"If Wager finds out, he'll have a shit fit."

"Fine with me. I need a complaint this month to fill my quota. Come on, your limo awaits."

"Thanks, Neal."

During the ride we talked about old times and new times, and I found out that there were still ten or twelve guys in the seven-eight who were there when I left, four years before.

"I'm trying to get out myself. I just keep applying for a transfer. Sooner or later I'll get it."

When he dropped me in front of my building, I wished him luck with his transfer and thanked him for the ride.

"Nicky D.," he said, gave me a little salute, and drove off.

Most of the people I knew from my old neighborhood still called me Nicky D., and a few of the guys I went through the academy with, like Neal. My father and sister just called me

Nicky, while my brother called me Nick. I called him "Father Vinnie." My brother the priest was the pride and joy of my family. Needless to say, I was sort of a black sheep.

When I got upstairs, the phone was ringing. I ran for it, even though I knew that nine times out of ten I picked it up on the last ring and got pissed because there was nobody there.

This was the tenth time.

"Nicky."

It was my sister, Maria.

"Hi, sugar."

"How's my big brother?"

"I'm fine."

"Keeping your trench coat clean?"

"All three of them, and my holster is well oiled."

It was an old routine. My sister was actually thrilled that I was a P.I. She was addicted to old movies.

"Nicky, I called to tell you . . ."

"What, Sis?"

"I'm . . . going away for a while."

"Going away? Where. For how long?"

"I—a week, I guess. I'm taking a plane today."

"To where?"

"I don't know. I've always wanted to see Greece . . ."

"Is he going with you?"

"He" was her husband, Peter Geller, who none of us liked for our own reasons. My old man, Vito, hated him because he wasn't Italian. Father Vinnie didn't like him because he wasn't Catholic. I didn't care for him because he was an asshole. I usually referred to him as "Numbnuts," but not so's my sister could hear.

"No, Peter is not coming . . ." she said, and her voice caught in her throat.

"Sis, what's wrong?"

36

"I just have to go away for a while, Nicky, and I wanted to let you know."

"Let's talk—"

"Not this time, Nicky," she said. "This time I have to handle it myself and not go running to my big brother."

"Maria—"

"I'll call you."

"Maria!" I said, but she'd hung up. "Damn it!"

She was a big girl, my sister, all of twenty-four, eight years younger than me and ten years younger than Father Vinnie. She was my father's baby, I was sure he'd know something—I just wasn't sure he'd tell me.

6

I dialed my father's number, and he answered on the second ring.

"Pop, it's Nick."

"Nicky, my boy, whatayousay?"

"Pop, what's going on with Maria? I just got a strange call from her."

"That somonabitch!" my father said. When he got his Sicilian up, his Italian accent became thicker and harder for him to handle.

"Are we talking about Peter, Pop?"

He said something in Italian.

"Pop, you know I can't understand you when you do that."

Father Vinnie spoke Italian, but I was never able to get the hang of it beyond a few choice curse words.

"Your sister, she's-a not happy, Nicky. She's-a goin' away to think."

"About what?"

"Her marriage."

"She's only been married a year. What's the matter with her marriage?"

"Who knows?"

"Maybe I should talk to Numbn—uh, Peter—"

"I already talked to him," he said, and I could sense my father trying to calm himself down. He stopped talking like Mamma Leone. "He says he can't make her happy for some reason."

"You knew she was going?"

"She told me yesterday."

"Did she talk to Father Vinnie?"

"You know your brother and sister can't talk, Nicky. They yell."

"Well, shit, Pop, we can't just let her go."

"She's a big girl, Nicky," my father said. "She said she wants to handle this herself."

"What airline?"

"She didn't tell me."

I would never call my father a liar to his face—but then we were on the phone, weren't we?

"Come on, Pop—"

"She made me promise, Nicky."

"Pop—"

"She'll be all right, Nicky. Listen to your father."

I closed my eyes and said, "Okay, Pop."

"So, when you comin' out to have dinner with your old man?"

"Out" was Bensonhurst, where my father still lived. The old

39

neighborhood. My father had lived there ever since he had come to this country from Italy forty years ago and started working on the Brooklyn docks. He'd retired two years ago and now spent his time going to ball games, the race track, and bitching that his kids never came to see him. Hell, he was never home!

"Soon, Pop, soon."

"You get hit onna head lately?"

"No, Pop."

"I don't know why you wanna work on a job where you get hit onna head a lot."

"Pop, you been watching 'Rockford Files' reruns again. I'll call you when I'm coming out, maybe later this week."

"Sure, sure, Nicky," he said, "I hold my breath. See ya."

"See ya, Pop."

As I hung up, there was a knock on the door. I must have had a puzzled look on my face because as soon as I opened it, Samantha Karson asked, "What's the matter with you?"

The building was set up so that there were two apartments on each floor, and Sam was my neighbor from the other side of the hall.

Sam's an extremely pretty cornflower blonde with very light eyebrows and eyelids—sort of like Sissy Spacek—and the most startling blue eyes I've ever seen.

To date she'd published three novels and about a half a dozen short stories in the romance field, but she always felt that my occupation might be fodder for that something else, so we talked a lot. We were good friends, had shared a lot of meals and pleasant times but not much else—and I'd be hard put to say why not.

"Why?" I asked in reply to her question.

"You look bemused."

"'Bemused,'" I repeated. "That's a writer's word, isn't it?

One that you use when you don't want to say 'puzzled' or 'confused'?"

"They're not all exactly the same. Which *are* you?"

"All three," I said, backing away from the door. "Come on in."

She was wearing a yellow T-shirt which said "Romantic Times" on it, whatever that was or meant. It was tight and tucked into tight jeans and showed off her full breasts very nicely. She was barefoot, which meant she'd come from her apartment and not from outside. I thought briefly of Jodi Hayworth and her tank top. Sam didn't wear tank tops, but my guess was that if she did, she'd stop a lot of traffic.

"What has you in this mood?" she asked.

"I just got off the phone with my sister, and then my father."

"That sweet old man," she said, smiling fondly. Sam and my dad had met on more than one occasion, and they were impressed with each other.

"That sweet old man," I said, "would gladly jump your bones, given half a chance."

"I know," she said, still smiling. "That sweet old man. What did he do to confuse you?"

"He and my sister both. She's flying off somewhere, and he won't tell me when or where."

"She didn't say where?"

"She said something about Greece, but who knows?"

"Your Pop, from what you say. Why wouldn't he tell you, though?"

"Because Maria asked him not to."

"And why would she do that?"

"She said something about wanting to solve her own problems without running to her big brother."

"Well, that's good. From what I know of your sister, it's time she tried that."

41

Sam had met Maria only once, when we'd gone to my dad's for Thanksgiving. She had met Peter, too, and also thought he was an asshole.

"I don't like it," I said, frowning.

"She's a big girl, Nick. Why don't you concentrate on your business instead of your sister's?"

"I don't have any business right now."

"Nick?"

"Yeah?"

Frowning, she tugged my shorts out of my pocket and held them up like a flag of truce.

"Why is your underwear in your back pocket?"

"Uh, there's a story behind that."

"So, tell it to me? It'll help you stop worrying about your sister."

I took my shorts out of her hand, and said, "You're just trying to pump me again."

"Well, I came over to invite you to dinner, on me," she said, folding her arms over her breasts. "Isn't that worth being pumped?"

"I don't know. What are we eating?"

"Chinese," she said, and then, "Szechuan. I've got it in my apartment, along with the rest of your laundry. Mrs. Goldstein left it off."

"That sweet old lady."

She grinned and said, "That sweet old lady would jump *your* bones if she had half a chance."

"Now, now . . ."

"Maybe we should introduce her to your father, and they could jump each other's bones?"

"Come on," I said, dropping my shorts back on the couch and grabbing her arm, "I don't like cold Chinese food."

"Will you tell me the story?"

"Does my Chinese food depend on it?"

42

She nodded and added, "And your underwear."

"Well, in that case," I said, moving her toward the door, "once upon a time there was this hole thing . . ."

"Wasn't it kind of dumb to leave him your card?" Sam asked.

We'd finished our Chinese food just about the time I finished my story, and were now working on a pot of coffee. Sam didn't cook, but she had mastered what she called "the art of Mr. Coffee."

"I didn't have any phony ones with me." The excuse sounded lame even to my ears. It was dumb to leave the man my real card, but who knew he was going to get killed?

"Well, what do you intend to do now?"

"About what?"

"About the man who got killed."

"Nothing."

"What do you mean, nothing? Aren't you going to try and find out who killed him?"

"What for? It's none of my business."

Her mouth opened once without any sound coming out, and then she tried again.

"Nick, aren't you a suspect?"

"Not really, Sam. Wager knows me well enough to know I wouldn't murder a man after presenting him with my card. Besides, nobody's paying me to find out who killed the old man."

She poured herself another cup of coffee and then said, "This would never work in a book."

"Why not?"

"Fictional private eyes have a code of ethics. They work on cases whether they're being paid or not."

"Why?"

"Why?" she repeated. "Uh, because that's what they do, that's why."

"That's because fictional private eyes don't have to eat."

43

We'd eaten off her living-room coffee table, sitting on the floor, and my knees cracked as I stood.

"Jesus . . ." I said, straightening up. "Thanks for dinner, Sam."

"Where are you going now?"

"Not out, if that's what you mean. I'm going into my apartment and put my feet up. I had a good week, but I don't have any cases right now—and I don't need one."

"But here you've got a murder to solve—"

"The police have a murder to solve, Sam," I said, correcting her, "and they wouldn't like me sticking my nose where it doesn't belong."

She walked me to the door, brooding.

"I'm sorry to disappoint you, Sam," I said as I opened the door. "Philip Marlowe I ain't."

"That's okay," she said. "You've got one thing over old Phil."

"What's that?"

"You're alive." She stretched up and kissed me on the cheek. When she did that her left breast pressed firmly against my arm, making me wonder again why I always ended up going back to my own place. "G'night, Nick."

"'Night, Sammy."

She swatted me on the shoulder as I went out the door. She hates it when I call her Sammy.

That is, she *says* she does.

Five days passed and I didn't hear from the cops again. I kept an eye on the papers to see if they'd solved the Hockshop Murder—which was what the newspapers were calling it—but there was nothing.

As for my own business, I picked up one case that took me two days of surveillance to solve. My business brought in enough for a single guy to live on, and since I had no in-

tentions of getting married in the near—or not so near—
future, I was satisfied with working one case that week. In fact,
four such cases—involving two days of work—at two hundred
a day plus expenses—and cheap at the price—were enough to
pay my rent and bills and leave some left over to eat and play
an occasional exacta at OTB.

Six days after my sister had left town I was sitting in my
office going over a *Racing Form*. I still didn't know exactly
why she had left or where she had gone, but then I hadn't yet
gotten a chance to go out and see my dad. When the phone
rang I would never have guessed what news it was bringing
me.

"Delvecchio."

"Nick—"

"Father Vinnie, hey!" It only took one word for me to know
my brother's voice, especially when that one word was my
name. "Whataya say?"

"Nick . . ." he said again, and this time one word was
enough for me to tell that something was wrong.

"What's wrong, Vinnie?" I asked. "Is it Pop?"

"No, it's not Pop," he said. "Nick, it's Maria."

"Maria? What's the matter with Maria?"

"Nick . . ."

"God damn it, Vinnie!" I said, forgetting that I was talking
to a priest. "Stop saying my name and tell me what's going on!"

"I don't know how to put it."

"Just say it, Father."

"Nick, Maria—she's been hijacked!"

7

He'd put it wrong.

It wasn't that Maria had been hijacked, but the *plane* she was on had been. She'd gone to Greece after all, but on the way back her flight had been grabbed by terrorists.

"That's what we got so far from the T.V., Nick," my brother said. "They're not even sure yet who the people are who took the plane."

"Are you sure about this, Vinnie? I mean, how do you know she was even on the plane?"

"Pop knew her flight."

"Pop knew a lot more than he was telling."

Vinnie agreed. "He always covered for her."

46

"Do we know for sure that she was on it? Maybe she missed it."

"We can't be sure either way, Nick," Vinnie said, "not until the authorities release the names, but Pop called her hotel, and they said she checked out."

"That doesn't mean she's on the plane. Where are you calling from?"

"Pop's house."

"I'll be right there, Vin."

I hung up and rushed across the hall to Sam's, hoping she was there. Luckily, she was.

"Sam—"

"What is it, Nick?"

"I need your car."

She knew immediately that whatever was wrong, it was serious.

"Sure, let me get the keys."

She left the door open and I stepped inside, then back outside, feeling numb. I didn't quite know where to stand. She came back with the keys and handed them to me.

"Nick, what's wrong?"

"Maria," I said, "her plane's been hijacked."

She caught her breath and then stared accusingly at her T.V., which was off. There was a small dot of light in the center of the screen, though, which indicated that she'd been watching when I knocked.

"You mean, the plane on the news—"

"All I know is what my brother told me on the phone, Sam. I haven't seen the news."

"Where are you going?"

"My father's house."

"Give me the keys," she said, snatching them out of my hand.

"What—"

"I'll fill you in on what I know on the way," she said, grabbing her purse.

"Sam—"

"Besides," she added, "you're in no condition to drive. I can see it in your eyes. You'll probably wrap yourself—and my car—around a tree."

She was right about that. My heart was beating a mile a minute, and my eyes felt hot and dry. I knew that her concern was for me, and not her car.

"Let's go, then."

My father lived on Ovington Avenue, which was also Sixty-eighth Street, between Fourteenth and Fifteenth Avenues. Some people called this section Bensonhurst, but on the map it said Borough Park. His house—the house I'd grown up in—is a one-family wood frame, semiattached on one side. The shingles were the same ugly green they'd been when I was a kid. The houses on the block were basically the same, with a two- or three-family brick thrown in every so often, like cavities. Like so many South Brooklyn blocks, this one was packed with homes, at least fifty-five of them.

I started to feel hemmed in as soon as Sam turned her car into the block. I felt like I had more room to breathe in an apartment on a block of brownstones than on a block like this.

Bad news travels fast. You had only to walk into my father's place to see that.

"What the hell are they doing here?" I asked Vinnie.

He had opened the door before we even reached it. We hadn't seen each other in weeks, but when we clasped hands tightly, it was for more reasons than just that.

"Nick, they all came as soon as they heard," my brother said.

The house was filled with neighbors sitting around as if it was a wake, a good dozen or so of them. I felt myself growing angrier by the minute. My sister had been hijacked—maybe—but, by God, she wasn't dead! They were sitting around like they were waiting for news that she was.

"Nick—" Vinnie said, maintaining his hold on my hand. Sam had noticed the panic in my eyes, and now Vinnie could see the anger.

"Get them out, Vinnie," I said angrily. "Get them out before I throw them out. This is not a damned wake!"

"Nick . . ." he said again, but then he squeezed my hand and said, "I'll ask them to leave."

"Where's Pop?"

"In his room. Hello, Miss Karson."

"Father. Can I help?"

"Just being here helps," he said. "My father likes you very much, you know."

"Nick, let's go see your father."

I left my brother with the job of emptying the house and led Sam to my father's room. A few people tried to catch my attention, but I marched right past them, ignoring their words, shaking off their touch. I'd never been the neighborly type, and I had no intentions of starting now.

When Vinnie said that Pop was in "his room," he hadn't meant his bedroom, but the sitting room that Pop had added to the back of the house. He'd built it himself when Vinnie and I were kids, before Maria was even born, and from that time on it had been "his room." He had a desk there, and a T.V., and a leather recliner, and he was in the recliner watching television when Sam and I entered the room.

"Pop . . ."

"Shh," he said, holding one hand up. "The news."

We waited and watched with him, but the report didn't say anything more than Sam had told me in the car. Flight 538 had been hijacked soon after takeoff by several terrorists, and as far as anyone knew, no one had been hurt. The plane was still

49

in the air while the terrorists were bargaining for a place to land and refuel. The nationality of the terrorists was either unknown or had simply not yet been disclosed.

When the report ended, Pop lowered the volume with his remote control and then looked at us.

If my eyes had looked anything like his, I was glad Sam'd had the good sense not to let me drive. I didn't even want my father to stand up.

"Pop."

"Nicky."

I walked to the recliner and put my hand on his shoulder.

"I'm sorry, Pop."

He patted my hand and said, "What do we do, Nicky? What do we do?"

"I don't know, Pop. I guess we wait."

He nodded, then looked at Sam.

"Miss Karson."

"Hello, Mr. Delvecchio," she said, coming forward. She crouched down in front of him and took his hand. "I'm so sorry. I'd like to help you."

He touched her face with his other hand and said, "You're so pretty, you help just by being here."

She smiled and said, "You're still a charmer, Mr. Delvecchio," and kissed him on the cheek.

"Ah, if I am such a charmer, then you will call me Vito, eh?"

"Sure, Vito. Whatever you say."

"This is a good girl, Nicky," he said, patting her hand, "a good girl . . . like my Maria . . ."

His voice caught in his throat, and I said, "Pop," because I didn't know what else to say. I'd never seen my father cry, not even at my mother's funeral.

"Nick," Sam said, giving me a meaningful look, and I gave

50

her a grateful one. I squeezed my father's shoulder and left the room.

On a table against the wall next to the doorway to Pop's room had always been a statue of the Virgin Mary, ever since we were kids. After Joey had been killed in Vietnam, however, Pop had hung a photo of him above the statue. I was standing there staring at it, maybe even shaking my head, when Father Vinnie came back into the room.

The house was empty and Vinnie was coming in the front door. My brother is taller than I am, six feet or so, and very slender. He is also better-looking than me, which is ironic, since attracting women is not one of his immediate concerns.

"I'm sorry, Vinnie—"

"That's okay, you were actually right . . . for once."

"Ha! Yeah." Couldn't resist a small dig, even now, huh, Father?

We stood there looking at each other for a few moments, my brother in his dark clothes and white collar that had made my mother so proud. I was wearing jeans and a short-sleeved shirt, and even though it was hot outside, I felt very cold.

"Jesus," I said, shivering suddenly, "is the air conditioner on in here?"

"No, Nick," Vinnie said, "but I know how you feel."

"Yeah, I guess you do," I said, and then I noticed something. "Hey!"

"What?"

"Where is he?"

"Who?"

"Our brother-in-law, Numbnuts, that's who. Where is that sonofabitch?"

"Nick . . ."

My brother had long ago gotten into the habit of speaking

my name and making it sound like a dozen words, all disapproving. I think they had a course in it at the seminary. "Disapproving Tone 101."

"Well, where is he?"

"I don't know. Pop says he hasn't heard from him."

"Anybody call his office?"

Maria's husband worked on Wall Street.

"I don't know the number."

"Well, Pop must have it in his book somewhere. I want that bastard here so I can ask him what he did to make Maria go off like that."

"Nick, don't fight with Peter."

"That's going to be up to him, brother. There's the book," I said, spotting it under an end table on top of a Brooklyn Yellow Pages. I grabbed it up and went through it, looking under "G." The number wasn't there.

"Damn!" I said, slapping the book shut. "He's got their home number, but not Numbnuts's business number."

"Why would Pop want to call . . . Peter at work?"

"That's a good question. I guess we'll just have to wait for him to hear about it from the news."

"Unless you want to go to his office and tell him."

"I don't know where it is."

"Pop does."

I thought about going to Wall Street to look for my brother-in-law and then said, "Fuck him."

"Nick!"

"Bless me, Father, for I have sinned," I said. My brother gave me a hard stare, and I said, "Okay, I'm sorry. Look, what do we know, so far?"

"Not much. The plane took off from Athens and was on its way to Rome."

"Why would anyone hijack a plane from Greece?"

"It originated from Egypt."

"Do we know who the hijackers are?"

"Not yet."

"You said on the phone that Pop called her hotel. Have you called anyone else?"

"I called the American consulate in Greece, and the State Department here in the United States."

"What did they say?"

"That the names of the passengers would be released at a later date. The State Department said they were inundated with calls and couldn't pick and choose who to keep informed right now."

I hated to admit it, but it sounded fair.

"The consulates in both Egypt and Greece said that they were working on getting a complete passenger list, and that the families of the hijacked passengers would be advised if the situation dragged on."

"Which means?"

"Which means that by the time they get around to calling families, the passengers may be released."

"If history repeats itself, Vinnie, these passengers are going to turn into hostages pretty quick."

"God forbid," he said.

"Damn," I said. "Vinnie, let's go for a walk." I needed some air.

"Where?"

"Up the corner. We'll get an egg cream."

"I haven't had an egg cream in a long time."

"Come on, Vinnie," I said. "It'll be like old times."

"Yeah," Vinnie said, grinning. "I buy, right?"

8

We left the house and walked toward Fourteenth Avenue.

"I wonder how Sam's doing with Pop."

"I'm sure she's doing fine. Pop speaks very highly of her, you know. He says you should marry her."

"Believe me, Vinnie," I said sincerely, "I shouldn't marry anyone."

"You're my last hope, you know."

I knew what he meant. Maria had gone along with Numbnuts and gotten married in a Jewish ceremony. I was Vinnie's last hope of performing the marriage ceremony for a member of his family.

When we reached the corner, we had to cross to get to the luncheonette that Mr. Canizotti used to run when we were kids. The front was so old there was a still a "Breyer's Ice Cream" leaf over the door—faded but readable. Mr. Canizotti had faded, too, about ten years before. I didn't know who was running it now, but I hoped they knew how to make a decent egg cream. Jesus, that was old Brooklyn: egg creams and stickball, Coney Island and Nathan's hot dogs and fries.

Right on the corner was an Italian club, and with the front door open we could hear the old Italian music coming from inside. That, too, was part of my childhood. This section of Borough Park was predominantly Italian, which was why there was very little street crime and burglaries. These people wouldn't call the cops, they'd solve the problem themselves. The petty thieves knew this, and wanted no part of the . . . Italians. If you were "connected," there was almost no need for you to lock your doors.

"Hey, Nicky, Father Vinnie," a voice called from inside the darkened interior of the club.

"Who's that?" Vinnie asked, peering inside.

"Sounds like Mr. Rosetti."

A small white-haired man shuffled through the doorway into the street, and we could see that I was right. Once, old Joseph Roselli was Joey Rose, a feared man in New York, but that was twenty, thirty years ago. Now he was just old Mr. Rosetti, seventy if he was a day.

"Hello, Mr. Rosetti," I said.

"Hello, boys. We heard about your sister. A terrible thing, terrible."

"Thank you, Mr. Rosetti," Vinnie said.

The old man put a withered hand on my brother's arm.

"Father, you tell Vito that if he needs anything, he should call us, eh?"

"I'll tell him, Mr. Rosetti. He'll appreciate it."

"Old Vito," Mr. Rosetti said, although my father was at least ten years younger than he was. "He'll appreciate it, but he won't call. A proud man, your father. He was much help to us on the docks in the old days."

I didn't particularly want to hear about that. None of my father's old friends—like Joey Rose, Frankie the Arm, and my namesake, Nicky Barracuda—liked it when I joined the police department. They always thought that "Vito's boys" would join them, even though my father was never really in the rackets. When Vinnie went into the seminary, they started to work on me, and maybe that was what pushed me the other way.

Pop did favors for "the boys" sometimes on the docks, because he was real popular with the dockworkers. They respected him and usually did what he asked them to do.

After I left the department, they offered me a job, but I turned them down as nicely as I could. I wanted to work for myself, I said. I'd had enough of working for other people. Maybe, they said, I'd be able to do them a favor or two, once in a while. Sure, I said, and maybe it would work the other way, too. Of course. . . .

"Anyway," Mr. Rosetti said, "you boys know you can call anytime, eh?"

"We know that, Mr. Rosetti," I said.

"Sure, I know you do. Uh, Father . . ."

"Yes, sir?"

"My Rosa, she not feeling so good lately. Maybe, uh, you could put a good word in? You know, with the boss upstairs?"

"I'll say a prayer, Mr. Rosetti. I'm sure the 'boss' will watch over her."

"You a good boy, Father," the old man said. "You both good boys."

"We're going across the street for an egg cream, Mr. Rosetti," I said. "Would you like to come?"

"I would like to, Nicky, yes, but walking across the street

56

and back would tire me out. Besides, since Canizotti died, the egg creams just ain't the same."

"We'll give it a try anyway," I said.

"Oh, they're still Brooklyn egg creams, Nicky, but Canizotti, he had the touch, eh?"

"He sure did."

"You boys go ahead. Give your father my best, eh?"

"We'll do that, sir."

He turned and shuffled back into the gloomy interior of the club, where he sat and traded war stories and lies with his friends and listened to music from the old country—even though half of them had been born here.

"Can you imagine that old man being one of the most feared hit—"

"I don't want to hear it, Nicky," Vinnie said, cutting me off. "Let's cross."

We crossed over and entered the luncheonette. The woman behind the counter asked us what we'd have. She had white hair, but despite her advanced age her face was virtually unlined.

"Egg creams," I said.

"Vanilla or chocolate?"

Mr. Canizotti would never have asked us that. An egg cream was an egg cream. I was about to lecture her on that when Father Vinnie jumped in ahead of me.

"Chocolate," he said. "Large ones."

We watched her as she made them, and she seemed to do everything right. The seltzer, the chocolate syrup, the milk, everything that old man Canizotti used to do—but no egg.

"Hey, no egg yolk?" I asked.

She stared at me, puzzled, and said, "What egg?"

"Never mind."

When she handed them over and we tasted them, we both made faces.

57

"Jesus," I said, "where can you get a good egg cream anymore, Vinnie?"

"I don't know, Nicky," he said, apparently taking my use—or misuse—of the Lord's name in stride, for once.

We turned and looked out the dusty plate-glass window at the laundromat across the street. It was filled with old women doing their husbands' laundry, not a decent pair of legs in sight. I almost said as much to my brother, but held my tongue.

"Nicky."

"Yeah?"

"Are you . . . do you ever see Nicky Barracuda?"

"My godfather?" I said, and I was using the word the way it was originally meant to be used. "Not really. He sends somebody around every so often to . . . feel me out."

"You don't . . . work for him, do you?"

"You asking me if I'm Mafia, Vinnie. Outfit, Syndicate, Cosa No-stra," I said, pronouncing it very deliberately. No real Italian would ever admit that such a thing existed. My father, for instance, wouldn't allow any of those names to be spoken in the house.

"No, I know you're smarter than that. I just don't want you to get in too deeply, that's all."

"I'm not in at all, Father," I said, and putting my half-finished egg-cream facsimile down on the counter, I said, "and I can't drink any more of that."

"Maybe we should have tried vanilla?" Vinnie said, putting his down, too.

"Then it wouldn't have been an egg cream. Come on, let's go back. Maybe Pop heard something on the news."

On the way back I asked, "How are things at the church?"

My brother was assigned to the Church of the Holy Family, in Canarsie, and had been since he left the seminary.

"Fine."

"They going to make you pastor yet?"

He shook his head.

"I'm still too young."

Both Father Vinnie and I knew that all he had to do was drop a bug in Nicky Barracuda's ear and he'd be pastor, bishop, or anything he wanted—short of Pope, maybe.

I wondered myself sometimes whether or not Vinnie did favors for Barracuda. The difference between my brother and me was that he wasn't shy about asking. Maybe I was afraid of what the answer would be if I did ask outright.

"Got to have one foot in the grave, huh?"

"Something like that."

"Hey, maybe the Barracuda could—"

"Nick!"

"I'm kidding, Vinnie," I said, hurriedly, "I'm just kidding."

We had half a block to go and walked the rest of the way in silence.

My father and Sam were still in his room, watching the T.V. There was one difference, though. My father was eating a sandwich, and there was a can of Bud on the floor next to him. When she heard us, Sam turned and looked, held a finger to her lips, and joined us.

"I made some sandwiches and got your father to eat one."

"How'd you do that?" Vinnie asked. "I tried to get him to eat earlier—"

"I charmed him."

"I can believe that," my brother said. It was an uncharacteristic remark. Sam seemed to have conquered all of the Delvecchio men.

"You guys better go into the kitchen and eat."

"Nicky?" my father called.

"Yeah, Pop?"

"Let Father Vinnie go into the kitchen with Miss Karson."

Vinnie looked at me, and I nodded. He and Sam went into the kitchen, and I went and stood by my father's chair.

"We saw Mr. Rosetti today, Pop. He said if you need anything—"

"Nick called."

I knew he was referring to Nicky Barracuda—Dominick Barracondi—his friend, my godfather, and boss of bosses in Brooklyn. I was "Nicky," his son, and his friend was "Nick."

"He says that all I have to do is say the word and he will send a team to get Maria."

"A team?" I said. "Jesus, Pop, you can't let him."

"He says as soon as they land and we know where they are, he can have a crack team—"

"Pop, he'll get her killed. Barracuda's men don't know anything about dealing with terrorists."

"Then you go," my father said, glaring up at me.

"Me?"

"Yeah, you. You the big-a-shot cop, the ace detective," he said, an accent creeping into his speech pattern. "You go anna save you sister's life."

"Pop, that's not fair," I said, feeling like shit.

"Fair! Is what is happening to your sister fair?"

Did he resent me that much for becoming a cop? If so, he'd never shown it before. Was it just his anger talking, or was his anger giving rise to his true feelings?

"Either you go and get her or I will tell Nick to go ahead. We take care of our own, Nicky."

Suddenly, I had the feeling that my father was more involved with the wise guys than I ever thought.

"Pop . . ."

"If your brother Joey was alive, he'd go."

That was his final shot, and I had neither the inclination or the ammo to fire back.

"Pop, I'll keep in touch."

I didn't know if he'd heard me. His attention was focused on the T.V., and he used the remote control to turn the volume up. From what I could see they were simply repeating their report of the incident.

I went into the kitchen and found Father Vinnie eating a sandwich while Sam was drinking coffee.

"Vinnie, are you going to stay around?"

"I don't think he should be alone, do you, Nick?"

"No, I don't, not in his present state of mind. Vinnie," I said, trying to choose my words carefully, "don't let him use the phone."

"Don't let him—Nick, what went on with you and him just now?"

I told him, word for word.

"He threw Joey at you?"

"Yeah."

Sam looked at me, and I shrugged. She knew that Joey, our older brother, had been killed in Vietnam in 1969, when he was nineteen, I was fifteen, and Vinnie was seventeen.

"That's not fair, Nick," Sam said. She got up and came over to me, putting her hand on my arm. "I mean, telling you to go and save her."

"She's right, Nick," Vinnie said, standing up. "You're not thinking of going, are you? You're not going to do anything foolish?"

"Where would I go?" I asked. "To Egypt? Greece? The plane's already gone from there, and it's still in the air. Besides, I don't know anything about terrorists. There are experts for that."

"You're right, Nick," Vinnie said. "I'm glad you're thinking straight."

"Vinnie, Pop's been watching Dan Rather. Why don't you give CBS a call and see if they can't tell you something?"

"Good idea. What are you going to be doing?"

61

"I have to go see Barracuda."

"Who's Barracuda?" Sam asked.

"Now that's not thinking straight, Nick." Father Vinnie frowned and looked disapproving. "What makes you think you can get in to see him?"

"Oh, I'll get in."

"Who's Barracuda?"

"My godfather."

She looked at me, unsure whether or not I was serious.

"What are you going to say to him, Nick?" Vinnie asked. He looked even more worried now than he did before.

"Save your worrying for Maria, Vinnie, and your prayers. I'm going to ask him to leave the situation alone. The only thing he'll accomplish is to get a lot of innocent people killed—maybe even Maria."

"You're going to tell Nicky Barracuda that we don't want his help?" Vinnie made it sound like he worked for the only authority higher than Nicky Barracuda. It was a throwback to our childhood, when we really thought that the Barracuda was God.

"Not in those words, but yeah, that's what I'm going to tell him."

Vinnie stared at me, and I thought that he was probably thinking about me what I was thinking about Pop only moments before. He was wondering how I could possibly intend to talk to the Barracuda like that if I wasn't in bed with him.

Well, I wasn't—but maybe I'd have to be in order to get him to lay off.

Maybe that's what he was planning, all along.

9

Sam wanted to come along, but I convinced her to stay. I thought my father would listen to her. She gave me the keys to her car and told me to drive carefully.

I drove to Fourteenth Avenue, made a right, went to Sixty-fifth Street and made another right. I followed Sixty-fifth Street until it met with Avenue P, then took Avenue P to Ocean Avenue. Once I hit Ocean Avenue, it was a straight run south to Sheepshead Bay.

My father's words had stung more than I had realized. When things were back to normal, we were going to have to sit down and talk about it. Was he in deep enough with the boys to have resented it when I enrolled in the police academy? And if so, why hadn't he said anything before, or even after the department and I had come to a parting of the ways?

Yeah, Pop and me were going to have to have a good long talk—after Maria was home.

Sheepshead Bay was a whole different Brooklyn, all the way at the southern tip. It was old homes, small wood-frame houses that used to be summer homes but were now year-round. A lot of them stood below sidewalk level now because they had been built before there was a sidewalk.

The main drag of Sheepshead Bay was Emmons Avenue, which was right on the bay. On one side were the docks, and if you got there later in the day, the boats were all in with their catches, selling fresh fish. The other side was lined with restaurants, most of them seafood places, the best in the city. On weekends there were flea markets in the parking lots, and the streets on both sides of Emmons were lined with street vendors.

This wasn't a weekend, though, and it wasn't late in the day. Kids were in school, people were at work, and Emmons was empty and quiet. The restaurants did a lunch business from nearby business areas. An island ran down the center of Emmons, and on either side of it there was angle parking. At the moment there were plenty of spots, but once it got on toward the dinner hour, there wouldn't be one to be had.

The air smelled of fish, garlic, and, from further down Emmons Avenue, knishes from a fast-food place called Shatzkin's. I parked the car and crossed to the bay side of Emmons, where there was a restaurant called On the Barge, which actually was on a barge. Needless to say, it was a seafood restaurant, but it was an Italian seafood restaurant.

It was also owned by Dominick Barracondi—Nicky the Barracuda.

The inside looked like the inside of a boat, with phony portholes and fishnets hanging from the walls, along with other paraphernalia like harpoons and anchors. The tables and chairs were oak, and so was the bar. Nicky Barracuda did not scrimp when he put together a fine Italian seafood restaurant—and that included the food. I'd eaten there before, and he had excellent chefs and used the best-quality fish and pasta. In fact, he had his own pasta made on the premises. The proof of the pudding was that Barracuda ate there himself, all his meals except breakfast.

They had a good lunch crowd and a maître d' on duty, and as I entered, the man turned to look at me. He was about eight feet across at the shoulders, dressed in a tux and flashing a diamond pinky ring on each hand. His name was Benvinuto Carbone—Benny the Card—and we knew each other. In fact, we'd gone to high school together.

"Aye, Don Cheech," he said, coming forward with his hand extended. "How's it hanging?"

"Like a noodle, Benny. How you doing?" He had a grip like a duck press.

"Fine, couldn't be better. Whataya think of the outfit?" He turned completely around, modeling his monkey suit.

"The rings are a little blinding, Benny, otherwise it's fine."

"You wanna have some lunch or what?"

"Lunch would be fine, Benny, but right now I've got to talk to Mr. Barracondi."

"I wish I could help you, paisan, but the boss is real busy."

"Would you tell him I'm here, Benny?"

He thought a moment and said, "Well, I guess I could do that."

"I'd really appreciate it."

"Hey, is this about your sister?"

"Yeah."

"Well, why didn't you say so? Geez, I was real sorry to hear about it—"

"Thanks, Benny. Could you, uh, call now?"

65

"Oh, sure, Nicky, sure." He turned to go to his station to use the phone, but then turned and said, "Hey, if he don't wanna see you, you're gonna have to leave."

"I'll leave."

"Okay, 'cause I wouldn't wanna have to throw you out, you being a paisan and all."

"Okay, fine."

Benny nodded happily and went to his station to use the phone. He dialed three numbers, said something, listened, nodded, and then lumbered over to me. Benny had always had the most unreadable face of all the kids who had ever beat me up in school. I didn't know now whether he was going to hug me or bear-hug me out the door.

"Whataya know?" he said. "The boss says he'll see you. He must like you a lot, Nicky."

"Well, why not? You do, don't you?"

"Not really."

I said we went to school together, but I never claimed that we were friends.

"But you're a paisan. Let's go."

"Lead the way, Benny, lead the way."

Nicky Barracuda was eating lunch at his desk. That meant he must have been pretty busy, which made his seeing me that much more of a favor. Nicky Barracuda dealt heavily in favors. One of his favorite mottos was "Tit for tat."

When I followed Benny into the room, Barracuda looked up from his clams and mussels and pasta and said, "Nicholas, come in, come in. Always good to see you."

"Thank you, Mr. Barracondi." I had always refused to call him "Godfather." It always made me feel like I was in a movie.

"Mr. Barracondi, you hear that, Benny?" Barracondi said. "This boy always did have the proper respect."

66

Benny didn't know what he was supposed to say to that, so he said, "Yeah."

"Yeah," Barracuda repeated. "That's all, Benny. Go back to work."

"Yes, sir."

Benny gave me a look I couldn't interpret and then backed out of the room, closing the door behind him.

"Sit down, sit down. You want some clams, some pasta?"

"No, nothing. Thanks."

I sat and looked at my godfather. He was in his sixties, a tall, elegant-looking man, almost like an Italian Cesar Romero. He even had the carefully clipped white mustache. As far back as I could remember, he'd always had the mustache.

"When you were a little boy," he said, "you used to call me Godfather. Then as you got older, you started calling me Uncle Dominick . . . then Uncle Dom. Now I am 'Mr. Barracondi.' I have not seen you for six months, Nicholas. In another six months will we be perfect strangers?"

"I don't think either one of us will ever be perfect, Mr. Barracondi."

He stared at me for a few moments and then said, "How is your father?"

"Not well."

"This hijacking?"

"You know that."

"Why are you here, Nicholas . . . after six months, why are you here now?"

"To ask you something."

"Ask."

"I want you to stay away from this thing."

"I can help."

67

"No, you can't help. All you'll do is get somebody killed. Leave it to the experts."

He laughed shortly.

"No one dies when it is left to the experts?"

"True, these things are rarely resolved without someone dying, but they know what they're doing. They've dealt with these people before. You have not."

"I have dealt with much in my lifetime, Nicholas."

"I know that—" I said, and then stopped. I was tired of being careful not to insult him, but I had to admit that I was intimidated by him.

"Mr. Barracondi—" I stopped again, then said, "Godfather, please, leave it alone."

"Ah," he said, raising his eyebrows, "*now* I am 'Godfather.'"

I didn't know what to say to that, but he saved me the trouble of floundering. He put both hands on the desk on either side of his seafood plate and pinned me with a hard stare.

"Let me see if I have this straight. You are asking me for a favor?"

Ah-hah, I thought.

"Yes."

He nodded shortly.

"I just wanted to get that out of the way."

He picked up his fork and twirled some pasta.

"Very well, I will stay out of it as long as I can."

"What does that mean?"

He looked at me quickly and said, "I will let the experts take care of it . . . until I believe that they *cannot* take care of it."

"That's not good enough . . ."

He smiled a humorless smile and said, "You are my godson when it suits you, Nicholas. That is not good enough for me."

We exchanged stares then, and I backed down.

68

"All right."

I stood up as he turned his attention to a clam.

"You tell Vito I ask for him, eh?"

"I will."

"And Father Vinnie? How is he?"

"He's fine."

"Still a priest in Canarsie, eh?"

"He seems to like it."

"You tell him to call me when he doesn't like it anymore, eh?"

"Sure, Mr. Barracondi," I said, rising. "I'll tell him."

I left, knowing full well what the visit had just cost me. I knew *what* it had cost me, what I didn't know was when, and how big.

10

I had another stop to make before I went back to my father's house, but I needed a phone first. I left On the Barge, got my car, and drove to a big diner down the road. Brooklyn diners always have breakfast twenty-four hours a day, and pay phones.

I stepped into the entry foyer and found two phones. One had a dial, the other had pushbuttons. Since I had been thinking so much about the past of late, I decided to use the one with the dial. I dialed the number of police headquarters in Manhattan—374-5000—and asked for Deputy Inspector Edward Gorman.

"I'm sorry, sir," the operator said, "the inspector is no longer assigned here."

"Can you tell me where he *is* assigned?"

"I'll connect you to Personnel."

I waited while the connection was made, and then a sweet female voice said, "Personnel, Police Administrative Aide Ingram."

"Miss Ingram, my name is Nicholas Delvecchio, and I'm trying to locate Deputy Inspector Gorman."

"Do you know where he's assigned?"

I bit back the first reply that came to mind and said, "No, all I know is that he used to be assigned to police headquarters."

"How long ago?"

I tried to remember the last time I'd seen Ed Gorman.

"I guess three, four months ago."

"I'll check."

The police department had not invested in Muzak yet, so I was left with a dead line while she did her checking, and it was anybody's guess whether I'd been cut off or was still on hold.

When I joined the department, Gorman had been a lieutenant in the seven-eight precinct. Three years later he was a captain in the two-four, but we kept in touch. When I left the department, he was a deputy inspector. Throughout all of that, he had also been my "rabbi," my connection within the department—if I wanted him to be. Time and time again he had offered to intercede on my behalf, first to get me a promotion, and then to keep me from getting kicked out of the department altogether. He'd had a lot to do with my getting the one-third pension and the P.I. license, although he'd never admit it.

During the four years since I'd left he had risen no higher than D.I., unless something had happened to change that in the past few months. Gorman had always been a man who spoke his mind, and that trait had gotten him to the rank of D.I., but it might also be what was keeping him there. When you have opinions and you voice them, you make enemies— and when one of your enemies rises a little higher and a little faster than you, that can keep you in one place for a long time.

P.A.A. Ingram came back on the line, letting me know that I had not been dropped into Ma Bell limbo.

"Sir?"

"I'm here."

"Deputy Inspector Gorman has been reassigned to the Brooklyn South Area."

I frowned.

"That's in the six-seven building, isn't it?"

"Yes, sir. It's in Flatbush. Snyder Avenue."

"All right, thank you."

"You're welcome, sir."

"Oh, one more thing?"

"Yes?"

"Could you give me the phone number of the six-seven?"

"Of course, sir. That's 469-7300."

"Thank you, Miss Ingram. You've been very helpful."

I hung up, wondering what Ed Gorman had done to get dumped into a shithole like the six-seven precinct.

The six-seven precinct building used to be on Snyder Avenue between Flatbush and Bedford Avenues, but when it turned one hundred years old, they moved everybody into a new building, still on Snyder but between Rogers and Nostrand Avenues.

Twenty years ago Flatbush Avenue was a shopper's paradise. Sears, Macy's, and dozens of small stores were always packed with shoppers, mostly women and their kids. My mother used to take me, Vinnie, and Joey with her whenever

72

she went shopping, and we'd have lunch in the cafeteria in *Mays*—as opposed to *Macy's*. Mays was gone now, and as I drove down Flatbush Avenue, the decay that the area had fallen into became more and more evident.

Over the years "the wrong element" had taken over the Flatbush area of Brooklyn. The streets were deserted now because people were afraid to walk, let alone shop. Oh sure, the malls had captured a lot of the shoppers who used to frequent the area, but more than that, people didn't want to shop where they had to be afraid they might be mugged, or their children might be threatened. (It was a common ploy for a street thief to approach a woman with an infant in a stroller and threaten the infant if the woman did not give up her purse—and that was if he didn't just knock her down and take it.)

A year before I left the department there had been a massive blackout in New York City, and that had naturally given rise to looting. The Flatbush area had been one of the most heavily hit by looting, and I had been sent there with some others to work the area. It had been like working a combat zone. I mean, under adverse circumstances even the most normal of people could give in to the urge to get something for nothing, but these people weren't normal. Iron gates had been ripped off windows so that they could get into the stores, and more often than not it had taken two or three cracks on the head with my nightstick to bring them down, where one would have normally done the job.

All of which I mention to illustrate what a hellhole the area covered by the men of the six-seven had become.

And D.I. Ed Gorman had been dropped into the middle of this.

Technically speaking, while the six-seven precinct covered the confines of the six-seven itself, the Brooklyn South Area covered all of the Brooklyn South precincts, many of which were not exactly garden spots and one or two of which were just as bad as the six-seven—or worse.

Flatbush Avenue south of Kings Highway was still pretty decent, but north of it—forget it.

I drove on Flatbush Avenue as far as Church Avenue, where Erasmus High School stood. Erasmus counted among its alumni Neil Diamond and Barbra Streisand, but it hadn't produced talent of that caliber for a long time, and probably never would again.

I turned right on Church, drove three blocks, turned right on Nostrand, drove two blocks, and turned right on Snyder. In the middle of the block the new six-seven building stood, a three-story structure of brick and concrete. I parked in front of a hydrant because summonses were not usually given out on the block of a precinct. There was always the chance that a cop would be ticketing another cop's car—or worse, a boss's.

I entered the precinct building and was approached by a handsome, black female police officer.

"Can I help you, sir?"

"Yes, I'm here to see Inspector Gorman."

"He's in Brooklyn South," she said. "That's on the third floor. Is he expecting you?"

"No," I said. I had called ahead to confirm that he was in, but had not spoken to him.

"I'll have to call upstairs and tell him you're here, then."

"Fine."

She did that, using a phone in an office to our right. When she hung up, she nodded toward the elevator and said, "You can go on up."

"Thank you."

I used the elevator without being decapitated by it and got off at the third floor. A handwritten sign was taped to the wall, with an arrow pointing to the right and the initials "B.S.A." on it—Brooklyn South Area.

I walked into a large room peppered with desks. There were four people in the room, three in civilian clothes and one in uniform. More than likely the ones dressed in civilian clothes *were* civilians. Even before I had joined the department, they had begun hiring civilians to do office jobs, freeing most of the cops for street duty. They called the civilians police administrative aides.

The uniformed cop was the one that approached me. He was a chunky man in his thirties with thinning black hair. His nameplate identified him as Officer Aiello. He had a small, off-duty revolver in a belt holster clipped to his belt on his right hip.

"Can I help you?"

"I'd like to see Inspector Gorman."

"You're . . ."

"Delvecchio. The desk called ahead."

"Right. Follow me, please."

He led me past the desks and a large Xerox machine to the back of the room, where he knocked on a closed door. A voice from the inside called out, and he opened it.

"Inspector, there's a Mr. Delboccio to see you."

"Delvecchio!" Ed Gorman called out. His booming voice bounced off the walls of the little room. "Get your candy-ass in here!"

11

Ed Gorman had had his nose broken so many times that it seemed to have ceased to exist. In spite of this, his face had a kind of . . . appeal, I guess, is the word. He looked like the sort of man you could trust. He was in his forties, young for a D.I., but if things went on the way they were going, his age would soon catch up to his rank.

He stood up and came around the desk with his hand outstretched.

"How the hell are you?"

"What the hell are you doing here?" The last time I'd seen him, Gorman was heading up the N.Y.P.D.'s Intelligence Division.

He regarded me for a moment and then said, "Did I ever tell you that I never had a rabbi?"

"You told me."

"I sure could use one now."

I didn't know what I was supposed to say to that.

"Want some coffee?"

"Sure."

He had a coffee machine on top of a filing cabinet. On a table opposite his desk was a color T.V. Even in a hole like this, rank had certain privileges.

He poured me a cup of coffee in a thick, white mug and handed it to me. He already had one on his desk, only his cup had a captain's shield stenciled on it. His wife had given it to him when he made captain.

"Black, right?"

"Right."

He went back behind his desk and sat down.

"Well, what the fuck are you doing here? I haven't laid eyes on you for three months now."

"You been watching T.V.?"

"On and off. What else is there to do here? Why?"

"You see the news? About the hijacking?"

"I heard something about it." He frowned. "You handling international cases now?"

I shook my head.

"Inspector, there's a good chance that my sister is on that plane."

"Little . . . Maria, isn't it?"

"Yes."

He stared at me for a few moments.

"Shit."

"Exactly."

"Shit, Nick, I'm sorry."

"I said she might be on it, Inspector. Nothing's been said on the news about who the passengers are, and I don't know that it will be in the papers yet."

He picked up a pen and began tapping it on the desk.

"What are you asking me, Nick—if you're asking me something."

"I am. I'd like you to try and find out for me if she's on the plane."

"How do you suggest I do that?"

I shrugged. "Make some phone calls, ask some questions."

"If I could make those kind of phone calls, Nick, do you think I'd be here?"

"You can't help yourself," I pointed out, "but maybe you can help me."

"You were on the job for five years, Nick. You were on your way to becoming a damned good cop, and I could have helped you, but you never asked me for it."

"I'm asking you now, Ed."

He rubbed his hand over his jaw.

"You're asking for your sister."

"And my father."

"How is the old man?"

"He's not taking this well. If there's a chance that she missed that plane, I'd like him to know about it as soon as possible."

"Nick, have you been out to Sheepshead Bay?"

"I talked to Barracuda, Ed, yeah."

"Did you ask him for his help?"

"I asked him *not* to help."

"I bet he must have appreciated that."

"He considers it a favor," I said, and Gorman gave me a look that said he knew what that meant.

When he began tapping his pen on the desk harder and faster, I knew I had him.

"All right," he said, dropping the pen. "All right, Nick, I'll make some calls and see what I can find out."

"I appreciate it," I said. I stood up and put my coffee cup down on his desk. I grabbed a pad and a pen and wrote down my father's phone number.

"You can call here. If I'm not there, my brother will be."

"Your brother the father?"

"That's right."

I took a sip of the coffee and made a face. "God, your coffee has gotten worse."

"Yeah," he said as I put the cup down on his desk, "I've missed you, too."

I drove back to my father's house and found the situation unchanged. He was still sitting in his chair in front of the television, while Father Vinnie and Sam sat in the living room.

"You've been gone a long time," Sam said as I entered. Vinnie and I both had keys to my father's house. When we suddenly realized that Pop was "elderly," we had insisted on it, and he'd given in just to shut us up.

"Don't worry," I said, "your car is in one piece."

"That's not what I meant, you jerk."

"I know," I said, touching her arm. "How's Pop?" The question was directed more at Vinnie.

"The same, Nick. They're not telling us very much more on T.V. than before. I guess we'll have to watch the newspapers tomorrow."

"Vinnie, can you stay here?"

We both knew that if one of us stayed, it would have to be him. Pop had always been hard on all of us. Joey had been his favorite, and after Joey died, he was even harder on Vinnie and me. Then after Vinnie became "Father" Vinnie—well, that left me.

"I can stay."

"You might be getting a call from Inspector Gorman."

Vinnie had never met Ed, but he knew who he was.

"I asked him to make some calls. He might be able to find out something about Maria."

"What about Barracuda?" Vinnie asked. "How did it go with him?"

"I asked him not to interfere, and he agreed."

"That's it?"

"That's it, Vinnie. Don't worry about Barracuda, just Pop."

My brother gave me a look that said I wasn't telling him everything, but then we weren't in the confessional. I was sure that when it came to Barracuda, he didn't tell me everything, either.

"Sam, I better get you home. You probably have some work to do."

I didn't want to see Pop at that moment, nor did I particularly want to talk to my brother. She took the hint and agreed that she did have some work to do.

"Father, if you need anything, please don't hesitate to call me."

"You've been very helpful, Miss Karson. Thank you."

"Nick, will you be by tomorrow?"

"Sure, early. I'll bring some breakfast."

"Fine."

There was a stiffness between my brother and me at the end of the day, and I wasn't sure if it was because of Pop or because of Barracuda. Maybe he felt I should have stayed, but some things had been said that I wanted to think about, and I couldn't do that there.

Sam drove back to Sackett Street and must have sensed that I wanted to think, because she remained silent all the way, right up until the time we reached our floor.

"Do you want some dinner?"

"I've got some frozen dinners in my freezer, Sam. That'll do for me, if you don't mind."

"I don't mind if your stomach doesn't."

"My stomach is used to anything."

"Nick—"

"Thanks for coming along, Sam. It meant a lot to Pop to have you there . . . and to me."

"Nick, some things were said . . . your father is very upset . . ."

"I know that, Sam. Believe me, I know that."

We stood in the hall for a few awkward moments, and then she said, "Thanks, Nick."

"For what?"

"For needing me, today."

And of course she was right. She was my friend, and I'd needed a friend.

I gave her a hug then, probably the most emotional moment that had ever passed between us, and then we went into our own apartments.

12

I was preoccupied with the events of the day as I entered my apartment and didn't become immediately aware that there was somebody there.

"It's about time you got home."

I stopped short and looked up. There were two of them, and one switched on a lamp. They were both big and brawny, almost identical but for the fact that one of them had a smooth complexion while the other's face was scarred with pockmarks. They were both wearing expensive suits, so they weren't just run-of-the-mill knuckledusters. If anything, they were well-paid legbreakers—but paid by who?

"Can I help you fellas?" I asked warily. "These aren't exactly my office hours."

"Well, that's fine with us, friend. This isn't exactly a business call."

"I'd really prefer you call my secretary for an appointment if you want to talk to me."

One of the men frowned and said, "You don't have a secretary."

"Now you've got the idea, friend." I backed up until I felt the door behind me, and then reached for the doorknob. My heart was pounding, because whoever these guys were, they weren't here to just talk, and I had the feeling they wouldn't just walk out when asked.

"I don't think you should open that door, pal," one of them said.

"Why? You want to go out through it? Or would you prefer a window?"

"A tough nut," Smoothie said.

"Tough nuts crack easy," Pockmark replied.

"Not this one," I said. I could feel the panic rising inside of me. I started to sweat profusely, and they misinterpreted that as a sign of weakness.

"Look at him sweat," the smooth-faced one said.

"He's scared."

"What do you want?"

"We want to know where the girl is," Smoothie said. He seemed to be the spokesman.

"What girl?"

"Jodi Hayworth."

"Jodi? I haven't seen her in a couple of weeks."

"Sure, that's when she came to you to hire you to do something for her. To find something for her."

I made no comment.

"You did your job and then she left, but you've seen her since, haven't you?"

"No."

"Look, friend, make this easy on yourself. All we want is the girl. Tell us where she is."

"I've already told you, I only saw her that one day."

"Tough nut," the other man said.

They started to move toward me, and with my back to the door I had nowhere to go.

"Come on, guys," I said. "You don't want to do this."

"You're right, we don't, so why don't you just tell us what we want to know?"

"All right," I said, my mind racing for an out. "All right, I know where she is. She gave me an address."

"What is it?"

"I wrote it down. It's in my desk drawer."

"Where's your desk?"

"In my office. Through that door."

They both turned their heads to look at the door, and I moved. They were standing close enough together that when I charged forward, I was able to hit each of them with one of my shoulders. One of them spun away and fell to the floor, but the other was merely pushed aside.

"Get him!" the man on the floor shouted.

I didn't know exactly what "Get him!" meant at that point. Most legbreakers didn't use anything more than a fist adorned with some brass knuckles, but I couldn't take the chance that these two might be armed with something more dangerous. If they had guns, they didn't even have to use them, just produce them, and then while one of them kept me covered, the other could administer a beating at his leisure.

I couldn't let that happen.

Not again.

I had a three-foot wooden coffee table set up in front of the

84

couch. It wasn't expensive, and it wasn't real heavy. In fact, with my adrenaline flowing the way it was, it hardly weighed anything.

As the standing man—the smooth-faced one—reached into his jacket, I grabbed the table, lifted it, and threw it at him. It cut through the air neatly and struck him in the stomach. This time he was knocked back and down.

I turned to the other man, who had risen to one knee by now and was reaching into his jacket. I launched a kick that caught him on the butt of the jaw, snapping his head back, and he slumped to the floor like a sack of loose shit.

Next to my couch was a small end table with one drawer. I pulled the drawer open, reached inside, and pulled out the slapper I kept in there. A slapper is a flat jack, carried by a lot of police officers because it is flat and fits better in the pocket than the cylindrical blackjack.

The smooth-faced man pushed the coffee table away from him and rose to his knees, one hand held against his stomach. With the other he began to reach frantically into his jacket. I literally ran across the room, swung the slapper, and caught him right on the forehead. The skin split as he went down onto his back and lay still, blood running down his face.

I sat down on the couch thinking about my gun. I don't carry it, even though I have a license, because I know that in certain violent situations I have a tendency to overreact. I know that about myself. If I *had* been wearing my gun, I might have made a move for it, and somebody might be dead—maybe even me.

There was a banging on the door that may have been going on for a while. I had only just become aware of it.

"Nick, it's Sam," she called out, still banging. "Nick, what's happening? Are you all right?"

I felt very weak and was fighting to catch my breath. I

wanted to go to the door and let her in, but there was something else I had to do first—if I could move.

I laid the slapper aside and bent over the man I'd just laid
out. I reached into his jacket and came out with a .38. I have a
gun something like it, but mine is in a safe in the floor of my
office. With certain parties eager for me to take a wrong step,
all I had to do was shoot somebody and that would have
clinched it.

Of course, I might have clinched it just now.

Holding the gun in my left hand, I checked the man out
with my right, looking for a pulse. I found one in his neck,
beating strong. His head was bleeding heavily because that's
what scalp wounds do, but he was alive.

I moved quickly to the other guy, reached into his jacket,
and disarmed him as well. Now if they woke up, they'd be no
threat to me.

I moved to the door and unlocked it before Sam could break
it down.

"What's going on?" she demanded, looking around. "From
across the hall it sounded like a riot."

"Some unexpected guests dropped in," I said, waving an
arm at the two men.

"Are you all right?"

"Yes."

I had a gun in each hand and tucked one into my belt.

"What did they want?"

"They wanted the location of a girl who I worked for a couple of weeks ago."

"Do you have it?"

"I have her home address, but I don't think that's what they
wanted."

The man with the scalp wound moaned, but he didn't wake
up. The other was still lying still, and it occurred to me that I
hadn't checked him out, only disarmed him.

"Shut the door," I told her, and went to do it now.

I reached for his neck, felt around for a pulse, then leaned over and pressed my head against his chest. I straightened his head out, but it fell over to the side again real quick.

"Fuck!"

I don't curse often—especially for an ex-cop—but I did it this time with feeling.

"Nick?"

I looked at her and said, "I'm in up to my neck, Sam. This one's got a *broken* neck."

"Is he dead?"

"About as dead as my license."

13

"What are we going to do?" Sam asked.

I looked at her and said, "I appreciate the 'we,' Sam, but you better get back to your own apartment. This is my problem."

"Never mind chasing me away, Nick," she said. "Make use of my fertile writer's mind. Let's figure this out. Do you call the police?"

"There's a lieutenant and some other police department officials, not to mention a politician, who would just love that."

"Why? Two men broke into your apartment, and you defended yourself. What can they make out of that?"

"Whatever they want. I'd rather not give them the chance to interpret this their way rather than mine."

"They'd really take your license away?"

"All they can do is call for a review, but with their recommendation I could very well lose it."

"Well, so what? Can't you go on doing what you do without one?"

"Sure, and so can a doctor, as long as he doesn't get caught either."

"What alternative do you have?"

Smooth-Face chose that particular time to stir, and I looked over at him.

"Maybe just one."

I went over to him and gave him a kick in the side. He moaned and rolled over.

"Come on, you're not hurt that bad."

He pushed himself to a seated position and put his hand to his head.

"I'm bleeding, man."

"You're doing a whole lot better than your partner."

"What?" He looked around and spotted the other man lying on his back.

"What happened to him?"

"He got his neck broken."

"You killed him?"

"You could look at it that way."

"Why you—"

He started to get up, but an apparent wave of dizziness had as much to do with arresting the movement as the gun in my hand did.

"You've already made a few mistakes, friend, don't make another. Besides, what was he, your brother or something?"

"No, he wasn't nothing to me," he said, holding his head. "Listen, you ain't calling the cops, are you?"

"What's the matter, pal?" I asked. "Don't you have a license for this?"

"Listen," he said, wiping some blood away with the back of his hand. "You ain't hurt, right? Just let me go before you call the cops. Whataya say?"

"I say you're right."

"What?" he said.

"What?" Sam said.

"Sure, why not?" I said to Sam. "I'm not hurt, so why make him suffer?"

"Yeah, right," the bloody man said.

"Sam, get the man a towel, will you?"

"Sure," she said, giving me a strange look.

She went to the bathroom to get one and I said to Smooth-Face, "All right, come on, get up."

"Sure, pal, sure."

He staggered to his feet and was getting his sea legs under him when Sam came back with a towel. She had dampened it and tossed it to him. He used it to clean some of the blood from his face and then wadded it up and held it to his forehead.

"Can I go?"

"Will you tell me why you were looking for the girl?"

"Hey, man, that puts me in an awkward position, you know? All right, look, we were hired to come here and ask you where the girl is. If you gave us a hard time, we were supposed to put a hurtin' on you. I admit that. If you're gonna let me walk out that door, I can't tell you who hired me. I wouldn't last two hours."

"What if I told you I'll kill you right here and now if you don't tell me?" I said. I raised the gun, pointed it at him, and cocked the hammer back. I felt Sam jump as the hammer clicked.

"Go ahead, man. I'm dead either way."

I had a few choices, then. I could try to beat it out of him, which I was not inclined to do; I could let him walk out; or I could kill him, and further complicate my life.

"Nick, give him to the police," Sam said.

"Hey, no—lady, don't tell him that."

She frowned and said, "I don't understand. You'd let him kill you, but you don't want him to call the police?"

"Lady. I got a record, and if you call the cops, I'll end up back inside for sure. I'd rather be dead than go back inside." He looked at me and said, "You understand that, don't you?"

"Sure," I said, lowering the gun, "Go on, get lost, but give your boss a message."

"He ain't my boss, we were just doing a job for him, but sure, I'll give him a message."

"Tell him I saw the girl that once, and haven't seen her since. That's on the level."

"I'll tell him," he said, staggering toward the door. "Hey, thanks, man. No hard feelings, huh?"

"Sure, no hard feelings."

As he reached for the doorknob, I said, "Hey, didn't you forget something?"

He frowned at me for a moment, then said, "Oh, yeah, sorry," and tossed down the towel.

"That's not what I meant. Him," I said, pointing at the dead man. "You forgot him."

"But . . . he's dead."

"And he's all yours."

He stared at me with his mouth open and then got it.

"Hey, now wait—"

"Look, pal, either you take him with you or I'll turn you

91

both over to the cops. He doesn't have to worry about going back inside the joint."

"What am I gonna do with him?"

"I don't give a shit what you do with him, I just want the two of you out of here."

He stood there for a few moments, undecided, and I prodded him a little.

"Come on, pal. Shit or get off the pot. Make a move. I can still call the cops."

Luckily, he wasn't that bright, or he might have figured out that I didn't want to call the police any more than he wanted me to.

"Is there a back way out?" he asked.

"I'll show you."

"All right . . ."

He picked up his dead partner fireman-carry style and started for the door. I opened it, and he preceded me out into the hall.

"Do me a favor," I said to Sam. "Find out if Mrs. Hanratty is home."

"Okay."

Mrs. Hanratty was an elderly lady who lived directly beneath me, and she was the only one who could throw a monkey wrench into the works. If she was home and had heard the commotion . . .

I stepped quickly into the hall and said to the man with the burden, "This way . . ."

When I got back to my apartment, Sam was inside, waiting.

"How did it go?" she asked.

"Fine. He'll probably drop him in a dumpster somewhere, but I told him to make sure it was at least a mile from here."

"What makes you think he won't drop him on the next block?"

92

"I told him I could still turn him over to the cops if the body turned up too close."

"Do you know who he is?"

I smiled and took something out of my pocket.

"I'm afraid Mr. Walter Harris is going to have to report his driver's license missing." I'd had him give me his license just before I let him walk away and dump his friend into the car they'd come in. I even played lookout for him to make sure he could do so unseen. He left without saying thank you.

"What about Mrs. Hanratty?"

"I rang her bell and knocked on her door. She's not home."

"Well, that works out fine, then."

I sat down on my sofa, took out both of the guns that had recently come into my possession, and put them into the drawer of the end table along with my slapper.

"Jesus . . ." I said, dry-washing my face with both hands.

Sam came over and sat next to me, putting her arm around my shoulders.

"Jesus, I was scared . . ." I said.

"You did all right for somebody who was scared."

I started to shake then, and she tightened her arm around me.

"Nick, are you all right?"

"Sure," I said, "sure, Sam, this just happens whenever I kill somebody."

"Oh, my God," she said, taking my hand with her other hand. "I thought . . ."

"You thought I did that sort of thing all the time, like in books and movies?"

"Nick, I'm sorry . . ."

"That's all right, Sam," I said, trying to control the shaking, "that's all right. I'm just glad you're here."

She held me tightly, then, and actually began to rock me at one point, holding me until the shakes subsided.

Hell, that's what friends are for, right?

14

O n the way to my father's house the next day I stopped at an Italian bakery on Eighteenth Avenue and bought a dozen pastries. Sam had wanted to come along, but I talked her out of it. She insisted I take her car, however, saying she'd be writing most of the day and wouldn't need it.

I let myself in just as Vinnie was coming out of the kitchen. I could smell fresh coffee in the air.

"Just in time," I said, holding up the box of pastries.

"Is that from . . ."

I nodded and said, "Malzone's."

"All right."

We went into the kitchen together, and he took down three coffee cups while I untied the box.

"Any news?"

"Yup. Last night after you left CBS had a report that the hijackers were Iranians. They routed the plane to Beirut, where they landed to refuel and make their demands."

"Which are?"

He shrugged. "I guess we'll find out sometime today."

"I hope so. Where's Pop?"

"Getting dressed."

"How is he?"

"I finally got him into bed at three, but he insisted on taking the black-and-white portable in his bedroom with him. He fell asleep about three-thirty."

"And he's up now?"

It was almost nine.

"He was up at six-thirty watching what's her name—"

"Joan Lunden?"

"Whatever."

He poured out the coffee, and I had the box open by the time Pop came into the room. I was shocked at how old he looked.

"Pop, pastries," I said.

"I don't want any," he said. He picked up a cup of coffee from the table and said, "I'll be in my room."

"Pop . . ." I started, but he just walked out as if he hadn't heard me—or hadn't wanted to.

Vinnie was sitting down with a cup of coffee and took a napoleon out of the pastry box.

I sat opposite him and chose a cream puff.

"Vinnie . . ."

"Yeah?"

"When I went into the police academy, did Pop talk to you?"

"About what?"

"About how he felt about it?"

He thought a moment and then said, "He mentioned something at the time."

"What?"

"Just that he thought you were making a mistake."

"Nothing more . . . demonstrative?"

"Nick," he said, putting down his pastry, "you're thinking about yesterday, and the things that were said. Pop was upset—"

"What about today? Right now? He didn't even look at me."

"He's upset . . ." Vinnie said again.

"That excuse can't cover everything, Vinnie."

"Talk to Pop about it, Nick, but after Maria is safe."

"Sure," I said, "sure . . ."

"What you should do is keep busy," Vinnie said. "I can stay here with Pop, Nick, you've got a living to make."

"Don't you?"

"Our situations are a little different. The church recognizes that I have a personal commitment here, but knows I'm also doing the Lord's work."

I hated it when he talked like that. It made me uncomfortable, and he knew it.

"Besides, if you stay here, all three of us are going to start getting on each other's nerves."

"You mean that I'll start to get on your nerves and Pop's nerves."

"Nick . . . I don't want to argue . . ."

"All right, neither do I. Maybe you're right, maybe I should keep busy."

"Do you have any . . . business at the moment, any cases?"

I almost said no right away, but then I thought about Jodi Hayworth and said, "Maybe I do."

"You don't know?"

"It's kind of up in the air. I haven't exactly been paid . . ."

"If you haven't been paid, why should you continue on with the case?"

I wondered what my brother the father would have said if I'd told him that killing a man the night before gave me a sort of vested interest?

15

P art of a priest's job was giving out advice, and although I'd gotten very little from that quarter in the past, this time it seemed to make sense.

After another cup of coffee and a second cream puff I told Vinnie I'd keep in touch and left.

In the car, driving to Bay Ridge, I went over that day and night with Jodi in my head. She had never given me her address, but at one point she had talked about living in Bay Ridge all her life, and having gone to Fort Hamilton High School.

I decided to start looking for her there.

*   *   *

Fort Hamilton High is on Shore Parkway in Bay Ridge, and counts among its most famous alumni New York Knick star forward Bernard King.

Jodi hadn't told me when she graduated, but my guess was that it was at least two or three years ago. To get her address, all I had to do was tell the girl who was working in the office that I was throwing an alumni party for those two classes and needed some addresses to complete the guest list. I gave her a half a dozen names, five of which I made up, the sixth of which was Jodi's. To my surprise she came back with two addresses, one for Jodi and one for the nonexistent—or so I thought when I pulled the name out of a hat—Charles Durning. I'd picked the name because I particularly liked Charles Durning the actor—I'd seen him in a Burt Reynolds movie recently—and as it turned out, there was a student by that name among the '84 graduating class.

Once outside the school I discarded the Durning address and looked at Jodi's. It was on Colonial Drive between East Seventy-sixth and Seventy-seventh Streets, about eight blocks away.

The house was a large, wood-frame, three-story, single-family house of the type that would command at least three hundred and fifty grand if it went on the market today.

I parked and went to the front door to ring the bell. My approach was to be very simple. I was looking for Jodi. Period. A girl who looked the way she did had to have a lot of men looking for her.

The door was opened by a woman who was so obviously Jodi's mother it was uncanny, even though she didn't yet look forty. She had the same blonde hair and the same lithe figure, although Jodi's mother was a little bustier than Jodi was. If the mother was any indication of what the daughter would look like later, a man could do worse than hook up with Jodi for the next twenty years or so.

"Yes?" she said.

"Mrs. Hayworth?"

"I'm Mrs. Ponzoni," the woman said, confusing me, but she cleared it up quick enough. "My first husband's name was Hayworth, though."

"Of course, I'm sorry," I said. "My name is Delvecchio and I'm looking for Jodi."

"Jodi?" she said quickly. "Have you seen her? Is she all right?"

"I'm sorry—"

"You see, we recently came back from abroad and we haven't seen Jodi yet."

I was about to explain that I had seen her about two weeks before when a man came up behind the woman. He was tall, dark-haired, broad-shouldered, and I'd seen him before. In fact, when Jodi's mother had introduced herself as Mrs. Ponzoni, I should have guessed.

Jodi's stepfather was "Tony Macaroni," a man who had once worked for Nicky Barracuda, many years ago. They called him "Macaroni" because his name, "Ponzoni," sounded like "Ronzoni," but of course they never called him that to his face.

When I knew him, I was about ten years old, and he was an enforcer on the docks. He probably would have known my father on sight, but he looked right at me without any sign of recognition.

The real test would be when he heard my name, which I had no intention of saying for a second time.

"Darling, this is Mr.—"

"My name is Nick, Mr. Ponzoni, and I'm looking for Jodi."

"She's not here."

"Yes, your wife told me that."

"Is she in trouble again?" he asked. The look on his face made it plain that he wasn't happy with his stepdaughter.

"She may well be, Mr. Ponzoni. May I come in for a moment?"

"I don't see why—"

"Tony," Mrs. Ponzoni said, and Tony Macaroni took a step back.

"Please, come in," she said to me, and also backed away.

I entered, and they led me to the living room. There were small statues everywhere: on the piano, on the mantel of the fireplace, on every end table and coffee table in the room.

"What's your connection with my stepdaughter, Mr.—"

"She hired me," I said, quickly.

"To do what?"

"I'm a private detective, Mr. Ponzoni, and what she hired me for is privileged, I'm afraid."

"I see," he said.

He was well over six feet and had stayed in condition over the years. There was a hint of a belly, and some gray hairs in the black, but he looked damned good for a guy who had to be almost fifty. The fact that he'd kept his looks had been why I'd been able to recognize him—that and the livid red scar over his left eye. He'd gotten that on the docks, during a strike.

He drew himself up to his full height now, as if it would intimidate me.

"Why are you looking for her, then?"

Here was the first time I really lied—and then again, it wasn't really a lie.

"Well, Mr. Ponzoni, I did the job your daughter hired me for—and believe me, it was nothing very serious, but she did leave without remembering to pay me."

"And you've been looking for her ever since?"

101

"Not exactly. Today I just seem to be trying to settle some of my old accounts."

"I see. How much did my stepdaughter owe you?"

"One day's work," I said. "Two hundred."

He nodded and was about to say something when his wife tugged on his arm and said, "Pay him, Tony."

"Diane—"

"Would you excuse us for a moment, please?" Mrs. Ponzoni asked, and I nodded cooperatively.

They left the room and had a rather heated, sotto voce discussion outside the door, and then returned with Ponzoni looking none too happy. I had the feeling that the former strong-arm man and enforcer was now a pussy-whipped husband.

As it turned out later, I couldn't have been more wrong.

"Mr.—what did you say your name was?"

"Nick," I said, intending to leave it at that, but before he could ask, I added "Delvecchio," watching his eyes very carefully.

There wasn't even the faintest glimmer of recognition—which meant he either didn't remember or he was very, very good.

"Mr. Delvecchio, my wife would like me to hire you to find her daughter."

"Well, I'm already looking, Mr. Ponzoni."

"Yes, but once I pay you what she owes you, you won't have any need to look for her anymore."

That wasn't exactly right. After what had happened in my apartment last night, it had occurred to me that Jodi Hayworth might be in deep trouble way over her head. Although I had no obligation to do so, I found myself wanting to find her and help her.

I didn't tell her stepfather that, though.

"You have a point."

102

"I will pay you the two hundred she owes you, and a thousand-dollar retainer to keep looking for her."

"That sounds fair."

"There is something else, though."

"What's that?"

"There is also a piece of artwork missing from the house, a statue about so high and shaped like a doughnut."

"A doughnut."

"I would like you to find that, as well. It may or may not be with Jodi, but perhaps if you find her, she can tell you where it is."

"Is it valuable?"

He surprised me by saying, "Yes, it is quite valuable."

"Was the house broken into while you were gone?"

"No indication of that. It's more likely that Jodi has the piece with her."

"Do you think she might have hocked it?"

Diane Ponzoni caught her breath, but her husband seemed to have already considered the possibility.

"Yes, it's possible."

"Have you checked with any pawnshops?"

"We only returned a few days ago," he said as if that explained why he had taken no action yet—if indeed he had not. Tony Macaroni had never really been the kind of man to let grass grow under his feet.

"Will you accept my offer?"

"Sure," I said without hesitation. Let him think I was in it for the money.

"Fine."

I expected him to go somewhere and get a checkbook, but he surprised me by putting a hand in his pocket and coming out with a wad of cash. He peeled off twelve one-hundred-dollar bills and handed them to me.

103

"I hope those are not too large for you."

"This is the kind of burden I can usually handle pretty well," I said, folding the bills and putting them in my own pocket.

"I will expect you to report to me periodically."

"Of course."

"Thank you for . . . for saying yes," Diane Ponzoni said.

"I'll find her, Mrs. Ponzoni. Don't worry."

"Thank you."

"I could use some names and addresses, you know, some of her friends?"

"I'll make a list," she said, and went to another room to do so, probably from a phone book of Jodi's.

"Now that we're alone," Ponzoni said, immediately, "I'm really not that concerned about my stepdaughter, Delvecchio. I am, on the other hand, concerned about that piece of art."

"I see."

"Don't judge me," he said without rancor. "That little tramp and I just don't get along, and nothing would suit me better than to have her move out."

"I understand a lot of parents feel that way about their own kids," I said.

"You're right about that. I don't have any of my own, and I don't want any."

"I don't have, either . . ." I said, and let it trail off as Mrs. Ponzoni came back into the room.

"I've written down the names of her closest friends, and their addresses."

She handed me a sheet of yellow lined paper with five names on it, and I folded it up and tucked it into my shirt pocket.

"I'll get back to you as soon as I have something to report, Mr. Ponzoni."

"Fine, fine," he said, giving me a look that said that we men understood each other. I almost expected him to wink at me over her head.

Outside I got into my car and took out the twelve hundred dollars. Nicky, you dog, you've taken money under false pretenses.

What would Father Vinnie say?

16

It was still early, and I had enough time to check out the names on the list. They were in Bay Ridge except for one, who lived in Manhattan, and they were all female. The four that I managed to squeeze into that one day were all flirtatious young things, and under ordinary circumstances I might have been inclined to make a play. Things were not normal, however, as the female who was occupying most of my mind was my sister, Maria.

It was after dinnertime when I finished with Jodi's four friends, and they had not been able to tell me anything helpful. None of them had seen her in a couple of weeks, and in fact, I'd seen her more recently than they had.

I called my brother from a pay phone to see if he and Pop had eaten, and when he said no, I said I'd bring something home. He said fine, as long as it wasn't Burger King or McDonald's. My brother was not the fast-food enthusiast I was. He did, however, like Chinese, and that was what I stopped and picked up.

When I walked in with the telltale gold-and-red dragon bag, Vinnie looked skyward and said, "My prayers have been answered," with uncharacteristic humor. It was then I realized that he was feeling the pressure as much as Pop or me. We were just all reacting in our own ways.

I carried the bags into the kitchen and deposited them on the table.

"Any news?"

"No, no news."

"Will Pop eat?"

"I'll take it to him."

"Vinnie, do you think we're babying him?"

"What do you mean?"

"I mean all he does is sit in front of the T.V. We bring him his meals, we put him to bed—all right, you put him to bed, but you see what I mean."

"Nick, Maria's his daughter."

"So, she's our sister, we're functioning, we're coping."

"He's an old man."

"You're making excuses for him."

"Come on. Pop's been through crises before, on the docks, at home—"

"Nothing like this."

"Vinnie—"

"I'll take him some food," Vinnie said, scraping a little from each carton onto a plate—some fried rice, some beef with broccoli, some lemon chicken. He started for the door, then turned.

"What?" I said.

"You're still sore at him for what he said the other day, aren't you?"

I didn't answer, and he left and took Pop the food.

I would have preferred to see Pop on his feet and in the kitchen eating with us rather than sitting on his duff feeling sorry for himself. He always called Maria his baby, and I thought I knew why now. His three boys had disappointed him. Joey went and got killed, Vinnie went and became a priest—which had pleased my mother, anyway, but my father had never been that religious—and me, I became a cop and *then* got kicked off.

Maria married a Jew instead of an Italian. Well, that was all right, she was his baby.

Her marriage was in trouble only a year after she'd said "I do." Well, hey, that was okay, because she was his baby.

Now she'd gone and gotten herself hijacked, and that wasn't her fault, but who was Pop feeling sorry for? Her? Or himself, because they had "his baby"?

Now, all this sounds like I've got something against my sister, and I don't. I love her, but of all the men in her life I was the only one who knew that she wasn't a baby anymore.

I had always thought that I got along with my father, but admittedly I didn't see him that much. Now, since this hijacking thing had thrown us together, we were getting on each other's nerves, and it hadn't taken long. So I knew I had been kidding myself. I stayed away from him because I knew we'd rub each other the wrong way. He called me all the time, but that was just his way of being a father. He never really wanted me to come out and see him.

By all rights this situation should have been affecting one Delvecchio, and the rest of us should have been feeling for her. Well, when Maria was back, there were still going to be things that the men in her life had to deal with.

108

And speaking of the men in her life . . .

"What about Numbnuts?" I asked as Vinnie came back into the room.

"Oh, I forgot to tell you. He called."

"He did? When?"

"This morning. He said he saw it on the late news last night when he got home."

"When he got home? How late does a stockbroker get home from Wall Street?"

"I don't know."

"I'll tell you how late. It depends on where else he goes. What was going on between him and Maria, Vinnie?"

Vinnie got two Buds from the refrigerator and then sat down to join me for dinner.

"I don't know," he said, handing me a bottle. "She didn't talk to me like she did to you."

"Well, she didn't talk to me about this. What about Pop?"

Vinnie made a face.

"Don't bother him with that now, Nick."

We were starting to rub each other the wrong way, too. Tragedy has a way of bringing families together . . . or tearing them apart.

"Is he coming here?"

"I told him there was no need."

"Well, maybe there is."

"Like what?"

"Like maybe I'd like to find out what made Maria leave."

"Nick, don't make one of your sordid divorce cases out of our sister."

"Fat lot you know, pal. I don't handle divorce cases."

"What goes on between a husband and wife is their business."

"Bullshit," I said, and stood up.

"Where you going?"

109

"A call."

"To who?"

"It's about a case I'm working on."

"What kind?"

"I'm trying to find a girl before someone else does."

"Is she in danger?"

"I think so."

"Can you help her?"

"A lot more than I can help Maria."

I walked to the kitchen phone and dialed the number of the Missing Persons Division of the N.Y.P.D.

"Missing Persons, Detective Siegel."

"Is Detective Reese working tonight, or Detective Hernandez?"

"Reese is here."

"Can I talk to him, please?"

Reese and I had come on the job together, and he had made detective when I was leaving. He was a go-getter—either that or he had a hell of a rabbi. Since I'd gotten my license, he'd done me a favor or two, and he'd introduced me to Hernandez. One of them was usually on duty, and that was helpful.

"Reese."

"It's Nick, John."

"Mr. Private Eye. What can I do for you?"

If there had been a boss around he would have called me "Mr. Nicholas."

"Just do me a favor and check your sheets for a blonde, early twenties—very early twenties—long blonde hair, very taut little body—"

"Taut?"

"Yeah, t-a-u-t, taut."

"Go on."

"About five-five, I guess, one ten or so, no distinguishing marks that I can remember."

110

"You fucked her and you can't remember?"

"I didn't say I—" I started to answer, and then remembered my brother in the room.

"You said no distinguishing marks that you could remember, you didn't say no marks that you could see. That means you saw it all, and that means you fucked her, and if you can't remember, it means you were drunk."

"Boy," I said, "you should be a detective. Do a thorough check, will you, and call me at this number?" I read off my father's number for him.

"I'll get back to you, Nick."

"Thanks, Reese."

I hung up and went back to the table.

"Do you always describe women like . . . that?"

"Like what?"

"Like . . . that," he said, pointing to the phone.

I looked at the phone, and then at him.

"I was talking to a cop, Vinnie, not a priest. I couldn't just say that she was pleasant-looking."

"Was she?"

"Yes, but—"

"Then why couldn't you say that?"

"Because I was talking to a cop."

"I don't understand."

"You never could." Before he could reply I asked, "Did you call CBS yesterday?"

"Yup, CBS, ABC, NBC, and CNN. None of them were very helpful. They suggested I watch their very comprehensive reports."

"Well, Pop's taking care of that, isn't he?"

"Don't start."

"Don't start," I repeated. I looked down at the food on my plate and lost my appetite for it. I wanted Reese to call me back so I could go out and get a quarter-pounder and some

111

fries, maybe even some nuggets. I liked them with the barbecue sauce.

The phone rang.

"Nick?"

"Yeah."

"Nothing on your dolly."

"No blondes at all?"

"Three women, all over forty. Two in the morgue, one in Kings County Hospital."

"Okay."

"Want me to make up a 'Looking For' on her?"

That meant that he'd file her description and if someone matching it did show up, he'd call me.

"Yeah, I'd appreciate it, John. Thanks for trying."

"Sure."

I hung up and turned to look at Vinnie.

"Does all of that mean she's not dead?"

"No," I said, "it means that if she is dead, she's still lying someplace."

He put down the sparerib he had been about to gnaw on.

"Vinnie, I've got to go."

"Where?"

"I've got to find this girl before she does end up dead."

"Are you going to finish eating?"

"No. Save it for Pop's dinner."

"Sure."

"Vinnie . . ."

"What?"

I hesitated, then said, "Nothing. Forget it. Take care of Pop. I'll call later."

As I started for the door, he called out, "Nick."

"What?"

"Are you going to talk to Peter?"

"Yes," I said, before I even realized that was the answer.

112

"Why?"

"Because whatever that sonofabitch did to Maria is what put her on that plane."

"Nick . . ."

"Relax, Father, I'm just going to talk to him."

"What's that in your back pocket?"

I looked down behind me and saw the handle of my slapper protruding just a bit.

"It's nothing—"

"I know it's not a gun because I know what a gun looks like, but I know it's not nothing, either."

"Give me a break."

"Are you wearing a gun?"

"No. Can I go now, Father?"

"Sure, go ahead. And do me a favor."

"What?"

"Don't get killed. As it is, Maria and I don't get along, but if she comes back and finds out that I let her favorite brother get killed, she'd never speak to me again."

He picked up the rib and began gnawing at it.

For want of something better to do, I left.

17

My sister and her husband had a two-family house in a different section of Bay Ridge than the one Jodi Hayworth lived in. Numbnuts had said that a two-family house was a "sound investment," so they bought one on Ninety-second Street between Third and Fourth Avenues. All I had to do was jump on Eighty-sixth Street, drive to Fourth and make a left, then a right on Ninety-second.

After I rang the bell, I started reviewing in my mind what I was going to say to my brother-in-law. I came up with three or four approaches—not the least desirable of which was to grab him by the throat—but I soon realized that he wasn't going to be answering the door.

114

He wasn't home.

My sister was in some foreign country under the guns of some fucking terrorists, and her husband wasn't home.

Grabbing him by the throat when I *did* find him was looking better and better all the time.

I stopped off on the way home and got a quarter-pounder, some fries, and nine McNuggets. I had the bag in one hand and my keys in the other when I entered my apartment. I didn't know which one to drop in order to go for my slapper, but when I saw who it was on my couch, I didn't have to.

"How did you get in?"

"Through a window," Jodi Hayworth said. "This place is a cracker box."

"Thanks. You hungry?"

"Actually, yes. Being knocked around makes me hungry."

She stood up then, and I got a better look at her face. She still had marvelous cat's eyes, but the skin around them was bruised, as was her bottom lip. Luckily, whoever had worked on her had not broken her wonderful nose.

"Anything broken?"

"Not a chance."

"Can you eat?"

"Of course."

"Well, come into the kitchen, then."

I led the way into the kitchen and turned on the light. I dropped the bag of food onto the table and went to the refrigerator for something to drink—cream soda, as it turned out. Dr. Brown's. By the time I set two bottles on the table, she was already chewing on the quarter-pounder.

"Hope you don't mind."

"That's okay," I said. "I like the nuggets. Can we split the fries?"

"Sure."

We dumped them into the other half of her Styrofoam burger box and covered them with ketchup.

"All right, start talking."

"About what?"

"I don't care what," I said, "as long as it has to do with the hole thing."

So she started talking.

17

The statue had been mailed home by her mother and father from Mexico, where they were "vacationing." They did this a lot, she said, sent things on home ahead, usually statues of some kind.

Jodi knew that the statues were worth money, and when she found herself in need of money, she decided to hock one.

"What did you need the money for, Jodi?"

"Is that important?"

"No, it's not important," I said, "but I'm the curious type, and I'd like to know. What did you need the money for?"

"I had a chance to make a good buy."

"Are we talking bikinis here, or drugs?"

"Just some coke."

"Uh-huh."

"You gonna lecture me?"

"Not me, I'm not your father. Just continue with your story."

"Well, I knew I was in trouble because this man came to the house a couple of days after I hocked the thing."

"What man?"

"Just a man who said he worked for my stepfather."

"Did he? I mean, did you know him?"

"I recognized him, yeah."

"So what did you tell him?"

"I started to lie to him and he . . . he grabbed me. He said he wanted that piece."

"Did he scare you?"

"Fucking-a he scared me."

"You told him the truth."

"Yeah."

"And what did he say? Come on, Jodi, don't make me drag this story out of you. I want to help."

"He said that I better get it back before my stepfather came home or we were both in a lot of trouble."

"Why both?"

"He was supposed to pick it up from me earlier, and that would have been before I hocked it."

"So his ass was in a sling with Ponzoni."

"Right. You say his name like you know him," she said, catching an inflection in my voice.

"I knew him once, yeah, a long time ago."

"What's he into—besides these statues, I mean? Is he Mafia?"

"Tell me your story, Jodi."

"Well, since I needed to get it back in a hurry, I decided to hire a detective. That's when I called you."

"Did your father's man—what's his name, anyway?"

118

"DiVolo. Carmine DiVolo."

I didn't know him.

"Did he agree with you about hiring a detective?"

"No, but fuck him. You got any coffee?"

"I can make some."

"You want that last french fry?"

"No, go ahead."

I got up and put the coffee maker on, then sat back down.

"Okay, so you hired me, and I got the address of the guy who bought the piece from the hockshop. We came back here, you popped into my bed, and then left—without paying me, I might add."

"I'm really sorry about that, Nick," she said. "Not about sleeping with you—that was fine. I mean running out on you like that, but I was looking to minimize my complications."

"Minimize your complications."

"Right."

I shook my head and said, "All right, go on."

"Okay," she said, wiping her hand across her mouth, then grabbing a napkin to clean both. "You got me the address, which was in Westchester. I drove up there, but I was too late."

"What do you mean, too late?"

"When I got there, the place looked like it was locked up tight. I broke in and found him."

"Found who?"

"The man who lived there. He was dead."

"How?"

"He'd been shot."

"And the piece, the doughnut?"

"It wasn't anywhere in the house. I looked."

"And left your fingerprints all over the place."

"I suppose."

119

"Well, where have you been since then? Your mother and stepfather say they haven't seen you since they got back."

"You talked to them?"

"Yes. Your stepfather doesn't seem to like you all that much."

"That's because I wouldn't put out for him."

"He made a pass at you?"

"*A* pass? He was always touching me and grabbing me. Once he walked in on me while I was in the tub, said that my mother wanted us to be a close-knit family—real close. If she hadn't come home, I think he would have raped me."

"Let's go on with the story."

"Sure. When I left there after searching the house DiVolo was waiting and asked me where the piece was. I told him I didn't know, but he didn't believe me. He dragged me out of the house and into a car with two other gorillas and they took me to a house in Greenpoint."

Greenpoint was a section of Brooklyn that, given a good push, would fall right over into Queens. My impression of Greenpoint has always been that it is a section of warehouses, although I know there are some stores and houses there. There's also a bar called Chambers' Pub where I've been known to have an occasional drink. The owner, Bill Chambers, has lived in Greenpoint all his life, and if I needed to know anything about the area, I'd call him.

"You've been there ever since?"

"Until night before last. DiVolo said they were going to keep me in ice until they found the piece."

"How did you get away?"

"DiVolo decided he wasn't as afraid of my stepfather as he thought and that it was time to fuck me. I had other ideas, so then he decided it was time to knock me around."

"And you had other ideas."

"I hit him on the head with a lamp and got the hell out of there."

"That's why they showed up here yesterday."

"Who?"

"Two men looking for you."

"Two gorillas?"

"That's an apt description, yeah."

"And what happened?"

"I convinced them that I didn't know where you were, and they left."

She looked dubious.

"Just like that?"

"Well, no, not just like that, but the end result is the same."

"So when they lost me, they came after you."

"And I guess they'll keep coming until they find that piece of art."

"I guess so. I'm sorry I got you into this, Nick."

"Well, that's neither here nor there. We're in it, and that's that."

"You mean you're going to help me?"

"Once we agree on just what kind of help it is you need, yeah, I don't see why not."

"Well, I need to get that piece back, that's for sure."

"And do what with it?"

A crafty look came into her eyes then.

"Well, if so many people want it, maybe I can sell it to the highest bidder."

"Like your stepfather?"

"Why not? He owes me for all the times he played grab-ass with me."

"Jodi, what is this piece of art really?"

"I don't know. It's just a round thing—"

"No, no," I said, shaking my head. "It's more than a piece of art. Your stepfather told me that he wasn't worried about you, but he would like to get that piece of art back. Your friend DiVolo wanted it back enough to snatch you, and those two goons last night wanted it enough to knock me around."

"Then what is it?"

"That's what I'm asking you."

"Jesus, all I know about it is that it's this ugly piece of artwork that Diane and Poppa Ponzoni sent back from Mexico just this last trip."

"Mexico," I said. "Was the thing hollow? Could there have been something in it?"

"Like what?"

"I don't know. Like drugs, maybe."

"You mean, I hocked the goddamned thing to buy some coke and maybe it was filled with drugs? Ain't that a kick in the head?"

"Look, Jodi, we've got to get this thing back, that's number one."

"And sell it?"

"I don't know. We'll decide what we're going to do with it when we get it back and find out what it really is."

"Are you saying you're in for a piece of whatever this thing turns out to be?"

She had turned suspicious on me.

"I'm in to keep you—and me—alive long enough to find it. I don't want any part of it once it's found."

That seemed to satisfy her.

"Okay. So, if that's number one, what's number two?"

"Well," I said, "number two may turn out to be number one."

"Which is?"

"We've got to find out who the Westchester police are looking for for this murder of—what's his name?"

122

"Uh, Berry, James Berry."

"Right, Berry. Anybody see you go in or come out of his house?"

"Not that I know of, except that DiVolo and his apes grabbed me coming out."

"Anybody see that?"

"No. I yelled enough that if somebody saw it, they would have done something."

"Yeah, well, don't count on that."

"Well, if nobody saw me go in, then I'm in the clear, ain't I?"

"Not if you left your fingerprints all over the damn house."

"My prints—"

Of course, even if she had left her prints, they wouldn't do the cops any good unless they were on file somewhere . . .

"Jodi, tell me you've never been arrested."

"I, uh, can't."

"Oh, fine. You were arrested for what? Wait, let me guess, possession of drugs?"

"Just a little bit," she said. "Poppa Ponzoni got me out."

"But you were fingerprinted?"

"Yes . . . but maybe he got them back. He's got connections, you know."

"You don't know for sure if he got them or not, though, so your prints might very well be on record."

"I suppose."

"Which means that the prints you left in this James Berry's house might be identified."

"Jesus," she said, "you mean the cops might be looking for me right now? For murder?"

"It's possible."

"Well, that's great. Carmine DiVolo's looking for me, my loving stepdaddy is looking for me, the cops are looking for me—"

"Why didn't you go back home after you got away from Di-Volo?"

"Because I wasn't all that sure that he wasn't working for Ponzoni, holding me because my stepdaddy told him to."

"What made you think that?"

"I don't know," she said, and for the first time since I met her some of the toughness went out of her. With her black eyes and bruised lip she looked like a sad little girl. "I didn't trust him. I don't know if I can trust anybody."

"Well, you better decide, because if I'm going to help you, you'll have to trust me."

She stared at me, lost control of her lower lip for a moment, then firmed up her jaw and said, "Is that damn coffee ready?"

"Yeah," I said, "the coffee's ready."

I tried to give her the bed, but she insisted that the couch would be fine. I found out later why she wanted me to have the bed.

When she sat on the bed, I rolled over.

"Jodi—"

"I don't want to sleep alone, Nick. In fact," she said, sliding under the sheet with me, "I don't want to sleep at all."

She was naked, and her skin was hot. I was wearing pajama bottoms but no top. The air-conditioning was on and her nipples were hard, scraping my chest.

"Do you?"

I wrapped my arms around her and said, "Hell, no . . ."

124

19

We attacked the refrigerator the next morning, and Jodi whipped up some potatoes and eggs, adding some onions that hadn't yet started walking around by themselves. Over breakfast we talked, and I got some more out of her.

"If DiVolo's not with Ponzoni, who's he working for, himself?"

"He's not smart enough."

"What kind of business is your stepfather in?"

"Import and export, or so he says. That's why they make all the trips."

"Did you ever hear him talk to your mother about a competitor?"

She thought a moment.

"Now that you mention it, he used to talk to my mother about a man named Janetti. He often complained that Janetti—I think his first name is Angelo—was trying to put him out of business, or put pressure on him."

That was a surprise to me. I'd been hoping that she was going to say the name Barracondi, or some other name that I'd recognize. Angelo Janetti was a new one on me. And then again, maybe Janetti really was a rival of Ponzoni's in the import-export business, and nothing more.

"Okay, now tell me something else. Has anyone new entered your life recently?"

"New? You mean men?"

"Yes, I mean men."

"Besides you?"

"Jodi . . ."

"Okay. I started seeing this young guy who lives in Manhattan."

"Has he ever been out to your house?"

"Several times. Why are you interested in who I'm seeing?"

"Well, Berry didn't have the doughnut, and you don't have it. *Somebody* has to."

"You think Terry's got it?"

"Terry?"

"Terry Jacks, that's the guy's name."

"Did Terry ever express any interest in your stepfather's collection?"

She thought a moment and said, "He may have picked up a piece or two to look at. Nick, the hole thing is missing from that house in Westchester now. Whoever killed James Berry must have it."

"You could be right."

126

"That would be DiVolo, wouldn't it? I mean, why else would he have been there if he hadn't killed him?"

"If he killed him, then he'd have the, uh, thing. Why would he need to grab you?"

"I don't know. What was he doing there, then?"

"Who knows? Maybe he shadowed you. He was probably looking for your doughnut piece of art, and I for one would like to know why."

"So would I."

"DiVolo was outside when you came out?"

"Yes."

"Do you think he was in the house at all?"

"Not then, not before me. He had his two goons hold onto me, and then he went in."

"How long was he in there?"

"Long enough to find out that the man was dead."

"What did he say when he came out?"

"He called me a dumb bitch and told his men to get me into the car. He thought I killed the guy!"

"Silly man."

"Nick, the hole thing must still be in the house in Westchester."

"You looked, Jodi."

"Maybe I didn't look good enough."

"And maybe Berry got rid of it before he was killed. Either that or whoever killed him has it."

"Then we're back to where I started. Whoever killed him has it."

"Guess so."

"Jesus, this is getting confusing."

"We'll figure it out."

She was silent for a moment and then said, "You know, you've never even asked me if I killed him."

"You're my client. I don't take on murderers as clients."

"He was killed *after* you did that job for me."

"Did you kill him?"

"No."

"Okay, fine."

"You believe me, just like that?"

"Yes."

I did, too. As far as I was concerned, Jodi Hayworth was a tough little broad who had gotten in a little over her head, and I was playing lifeguard—only in this case, judging from the visit I'd had the other night, the lifeguard's life might be in just as much danger as hers.

We stared at each other for a few moments, and then she asked, "Well, what are we gonna do first?"

"*You're* going to stay someplace safe. *I've* got to be able to move around and see if I can't find out what happened to the hole thing. I get the feeling we're both in a hole that only that piece of art is going to get us out of."

"You're going to Westchester?"

"That's a possibility."

"To talk to the cops?"

"No, I don't want to talk to the cops out there because I don't want them to know who I am. If they know I'm working for you, a logical move would be to watch this building. No, if I do go out there, it'll just be to take a look around. I'm going to talk to some friends of mine in the police department to see if they can't get me some information from the Westchester cops."

"So where am I going to stay?"

"Across the hall."

"Alone?"

"Sam's home all day, so I don't think you'll be alone. Come on, I'll introduce you."

"Okay."

As she got up, I said, "Oh, by the way."

"Yes?"

"How did you meet Terry Jacks?"

"Through Janet Jackson."

"Janet—that's a friend of yours who lives in Manhattan, isn't it?"

"Yes, how'd you know?"

"Your mother gave me a list of your friends, including Janet Jackson. I talked to all of them except her."

"Can I see the list?"

"Sure."

I retrieved it from the back pocket of the pants I'd worn yesterday and showed it to her.

"How about letting me have that card that we got from the hockshop?"

"Sure."

She reached into her pocket and handed it over. I refrained from telling her that the old man we'd gotten it from was dead.

"I don't even see two of these girls anymore."

"What about Janet?"

"She's probably my best friend right now."

"I guess I'll have to talk to her, then."

"About what?"

"About Terry Jacks. Why don't you write his address on the back of that list, too?"

She picked up a pencil and did as I asked.

"Does Janet have a job?"

"Of course. She works in a record store on St. Mark's Place. It's called Sounds."

"Well, you better give me that address, too. What about your friend Terry? Does he work?"

"He's an artist."

Did that answer my question?

"I should find him home, then?"

"Most likely. He paints during the day and goes out in the evening."

"He must have some other source of income than his painting."

"Oh, he's never sold a painting. He lives on an allowance from his father."

I took the piece of paper back from her and looked at what she had written.

"That explains why his address is much further uptown than Janet's."

Janet Jackson lived in an apartment in the West Village, on Horatio Street, while Terry Jacks lived uptown, an address on Eighty-third Street, between York and First.

"Why are you interested in Terry?" she asked, handing the list back to me.

"I'm interested in anyone and anything that came into your life recently. Somebody has this hole thing of yours, and somebody killed James Berry. I'm just looking around, Jodi. That's what a detective does."

"I'd like to help."

"You will, by staying out of sight so I don't have to worry about you."

"Across the hall?"

"Across the hall. Come on, I'll introduce you to Sam."

We started for the door, and I said, "Jodi, one last thing."

"Yes?"

"Is there anything that you haven't told me so far that you'd like to tell me now?"

"Like what?"

"Like something you forgot, or something you're afraid to talk about. Anything at all."

She thought a moment and seemed to honestly be concentrating on the question.

"There's nothing else I can think of."

"All right, then. Let's go."

130

Looking back, I guess it did sound as if I was avoiding mentioning that Sam was a woman. Jodi gave me a look when I introduced them, and then she and Sam gave each other those looks that attractive women do when they meet.

"Jodi, why don't you wait inside," I suggested.

"Sure."

She slid by Sam and went into her apartment.

"How's your father, Nick?"

"Shit," I said, "I didn't call him this morning."

"Well, you must have other things on your mind."

The remark would have sounded catty coming from someone else, but I'd never heard Sam be catty before, and I didn't think she was being so now.

"I'll have to call and talk to Vinnie before I go out. Listen, Sam, Jodi has something to do with those guys that were here the other night."

"She's the girl they were looking for."

"Right."

"Is that how she got beat up?"

"Yes. They had her but she got away, and they're probably still looking for her. I need to stash her someplace safe while I look around."

"For what?"

"I'll have to explain that to you another time."

"All right, I'll keep her here, Nick."

"I appreciate it, Sam."

"But I will get the whole story from you, won't I?"

"Sure—unless you can get it from Jodi. It'll give you two something to talk about."

"Oh, I don't think we'll have any trouble finding something to talk about."

I left, wondering what that meant.

20

I went back into my apartment and dialed my father's number. My brother answered on the second ring.

"Vinnie? How's Pop?"

"The same."

"Any news?"

"The terrorists have made some demands. They want the Israeli government to release Lebanese prisoners."

"What does that have to do with the United States?"

"I guess they want the President to intercede on their behalf."

"Jesus."

"There's something else."

"What?"

"They've released the names of the hostages that are still being held."

"Are *they* calling them hostages now?"

"Yes."

"And?"

"They've released all but twelve people, and Maria is among them."

"What possible reason could they have to keep her?"

"Who knows how they choose, Nick? There's something else going on here, though, now that all of the names have been released."

"What's that?"

"We've been getting telephone calls from *Good Morning America*, *CBS Morning News*, and from other stations who want Pop to go on T.V. and talk about this."

"What does Pop say?"

"He says if he goes on television, he'll use up time that could be used to report developments. He wants to stay in front of the T.V., Nick, not on it."

"Well, good for him. He won't be part of a media circus."

"But can the same be said for Peter?"

Our brother-in-law was no wallflower. Hell, he'd jump at the chance to be on T.V.

"I'll kill him."

"You don't mean that."

"Well, I'll let him have it, then. Take whatever phraseology you prefer."

"Did you see him yesterday?"

"He wasn't home."

"Where was he?"

"I don't know, Vin, but I intend to find out. I'll call you later."

"Wait a minute."

133

"For what?"

"Your friend Inspector Gorman called."

"What did he have to say?"

"Apparently whatever it is, he wants to say it to you." My brother sounded slightly miffed. "The only message he left was for you to call him as soon as you can."

When I hung up, I thought a moment, then took out my phone book, looked up a number, and dialed it.

"Bogie's," a voice said on the line.

"I'd like to speak to Miles Jacoby, please."

"Hold on, I'll see if he's here."

I could have tried Miles's home number, but he was at Bogie's more than he was at home. Bogie's was a restaurant in Manhattan on West Twenty-sixth Street with a Humphrey Bogart motif—posters, photos, black-bird busts, and "Key Largo" on the jukebox. Jack was a P.I. working out of Manhattan, and I needed him to do me a favor.

"Jacoby."

"Jack, it's Nick Delvecchio."

"Nicky D., how you doing?"

"Pretty good, except I need a favor."

"Well, I've got a few left. What can I do for you?"

"You're not going to like this, Jack, but I'd like you to follow my brother-in-law."

"Your brother-in-law? What's up?"

"Let me give you the whole story," I said, and I told him about the hijacking.

"Jesus, Nick, I'm sorry. Do you know how she is?"

"As far as we know she's fine, but I don't think her husband is as concerned as he should be."

"You think he's stepping out?"

"That might be the reason my sister went away, Nick. Things weren't going too well between them."

"How long have they been married?"

134

"About a year."

"What kind of fella is he?"

"He hasn't exactly fit in with the Delvecchio menfolk."

"Okay, Nick, you want me to find out if he's got a playmate, and then what?"

"Just let me know. If the bastard sent my sister running off on that flight because he likes to fool around—"

"Nick, easy," Jack said. "I'm not going to finger him for you so you can work him over."

"No, I wouldn't ask you to do that, Jack."

"I'll tail him for you, Nick."

"I'd do it myself, but on top of the thing with my sister I've got a girl's life in my hands."

"No sweat. Just give me the particulars."

I gave him my brother-in-law's name and home address and told him he worked on Wall Street but I wasn't sure where.

"You can pick him up at home tomorrow and go from there—" I started, but Jack cut me off.

"I can find out where he works. If he's fooling around, he might be doing it during business hours. Maybe I can wrap this up for you today."

"I appreciate this, Jack—and listen, make sure you send me a bill."

"Sure, I'll mail it, but you know how the mail service is in New York. When you coming to Manhattan, Nick? You can't hide in Brooklyn forever."

"As a matter of fact, I'll be in Manhattan today for a little while."

"Meet me at Bogie's before you go back to Brooklyn, say at four? That'll give me time to pick your brother-in-law up at work at five and follow him home. If I can't meet you, I'll call you there."

"Okay, fine."

135

"Just tell Billy Palmer, the owner, or the manager Stuart that you're a friend of mine."

"Will they poison me?"

"Probably, but it'll be the best poison in town. Now let's hang up so we can both get to work."

"Thanks, Jack."

"About your sister, Nick, if there's anything I can do . . ."

"Thanks again, Jack."

When I hung up, I decided to take his advice and get right to work. That meant going to Manhattan to talk to Janet Jackson and Terry Jacks, or going out to Westchester. The latter was a longer trip, and the possibility of killing a whole day getting out there and back did not appeal to me.

There was an easier way, since I had to call Inspector Ed Gorman anyway.

21

I hate going to Manhattan because it's impossible to take a car into the city without risking insanity, and it's impossible to take the subway without risking death in one form or another. (That might be an exaggeration, but if it is, it's only a slight one.)

I decided to take the easy route and simply walk across the Brooklyn Bridge.

On a good day—like today—the bridge looks like one side or the other is being evacuated. If it's morning, people are walking from Brooklyn into the city, and if it's early evening, they're walking the other way.

Today I was walking to the city with the young executives

with their jackets over their arms and their ties and collars loosened, and the young secretaries and women executives in their sundresses or linen suits.

As far as the women went on this day, the view was very pleasant, but my mind kept wandering from Jodi's case to my sister's predicament, back and forth like a goddamned Ping-Pong ball.

If I couldn't locate the hole thing, then Jodi would continue to be in danger.

If my brother-in-law was cheating on my sister, the sonofabitch was in for a hard time from me. . . .

How long would it take for the people who were looking for Jodi to figure that maybe I was the one who took the piece of artwork—and then they'd be after me, if they weren't already. That's what I had meant when I told Jodi that we were both possibly in a hole. . . .

And if I didn't have enough random thoughts flicking through my head to give me a headache, I kept thinking about Maria, my father's baby. She wasn't a baby, though, she was a grown woman with more backbone than my father or my brother gave her credit for.

I wondered how would the terrorists respond to an American woman with backbone?

To try and steady my mind before I got dizzy, I thought about the last call I'd made before leaving my apartment. After hanging up on Jacoby, I'd dialed the Sixty-seventh Precinct number, been cut off by an incompetent civilian on the switchboard, and then finally got through to Gorman.

"Ed, it's Nick."

"I'm glad you called. I thought you'd be interested in knowing that your sister is still alive."

"You know that for a fact?"

"I've got a friend in the State Department. He was able to

find out the condition of the remaining hostages. At last report, they were all alive and well."

"Ed, this means a lot to me."

"I'll try and keep an eye on the situation, Nick, and let you know if anything changes, but I can't guarantee anything."

"Whatever you can do, Ed, my family and I will appreciate."

"How's your old man holding up?"

"All right, I guess."

"Why aren't you at his house with your family instead of running around the city?"

"I'm working on something, Ed—and come to think of it," I said, doing my best to sound as if something had just occurred to me, "maybe you can help me with this, too."

"Come to think of it, huh? All right, then, let me have it."

"There was a murder in Westchester about two weeks or so ago, a wealthy man shot in his home."

"Yeah?" His tone was wary.

"I'd like to find out about it."

"What do you want to know?"

"*All* about it. What the cops have found so far, whethe' not they're looking for suspects—"

"Any suspect in particular?" he asked. "Like maybe ent?"

"I appreciate all your help, Ed. I'll keep in touc

I hung up on him while he was still talking. I taking unfair advantage of his willingness to help never asked for it when I was on the job. Maybe

I only hoped that he felt that way too.

22

I tried Janet Jackson's home address first, an old five-story brick on Horatio Street, near Ninth Avenue, but she wasn't there. It was a less then scenic block, filled with aging brick buildings and a park I wouldn't have let a kid near with a suit of armor.

I walked crosstown to St. Mark's Place, and turning into the block between Second and Third—which is also East Eighth Street—was like entering a whole new world, even for Manhattan.

The street was lined with shops and restaurants, many of which had sidewalk service. The people who inhabited that

block looked normal . . . in that they all had two arms, two legs, and a head. Beyond that, they were from another planet.

There were men in turquoise jumpsuits with pink hair on their heads—where there was hair. You haven't lived until you've seen a white dude—or girl—with a pink Mr. T mohawk and a collection of earrings that jingle when they walk. And then there were the leather-clad jerks with punk hairdos, stubble-covered faces and outfits unzipped to their navels revealing hairless chests.

There were hookers on the corner of St. Mark's and Third Avenue who approached cars when they stopped for the red light there. Further down the block was a hotel which was probably where they took the drivers who took their scantily clad bait. There were other gals just waiting on the steps for the johns to make the first move. As I went by, one of them lifted her tank top to expose her breasts to induce me to make that move, but I was less than compelled.

It was fitting that the Second Avenue Theater, just around the corner, was showing *Little Shop of Horrors*, and had been for some time.

When I reached the center of the block, I saw the sign that said "Sounds." A couple in matching jumpsuits came walking out at that point and I really couldn't tell if they were of the same sex, or even which sex they were. The place had huge windows, three of them, with a speaker mounted in each of the end ones. I had to ascend a flight of stone steps to get to the front door, which was made entirely of sheet metal.

Inside, an assortment of St. Mark's Place characters lined the two aisles of record albums, and there were even a couple of young executive types who had probably taken an early lunch to come down and shop.

The counter was way above floor level, probably so the employees could look down on the store, making it easier to spot

141

shoplifters. Behind the counter was a white guy with blonde hair that was cut so close he looked bald, and a stunning black girl with cornrows. She appeared to be in her early twenties, and even for one as easily smitten as I am, she looked like something special.

"Excuse me," I shouted over the music. Some girl singer I didn't recognize was singing about "baad, baad, baad, baad boooys" making her feel "sooo good!"

They both looked at me, and the man asked, "Can I help you?"

"I'm looking for Janet Jackson!"

I didn't know if they could hear me or not, or if lipreading was a requirement of their job, but the girl moved over in front of the guy and said, "I'm Janet."

I was surprised. Jodi had said nothing about Janet Jackson being black.

"Could I talk to you, please?"

"You want to sell some records?"

"No, I want to talk!"

I took out the photostat of my P.I. license and passed it up to her. She read it, frowned, and handed it back. She said something to the young man and then walked to the end of the platform and stepped down. That she was so short was another surprise. She couldn't have been more than five feet tall.

"What's this about?" she asked, putting her lips next to my ear. To do so, she had to press her full breasts tightly against my arm. Her breath was warm and pleasant.

"Jodi Hayworth."

"Is she—" she began, but I overrode her by saying, "Can we go somewhere?"

She nodded and beckoned me to follow her out the front door. When the metal door closed behind us, it became a little quieter.

"There's a bar downstairs," she said in an almost normal

142

voice. That was the first time I realized that she had some kind of an accent, probably Jamaican. "Is that all right?"

"That's fine," I said. "I'll buy."

We walked down the steps, made a sharp right, and walked down five steps to the bar. The front door was plain wood, and there was no name in evidence. As we walked in, the bar was on the left and there was a wooden partition, about chest high, separating it from a group of tables on the right. The crowd inside was a good mix. Apparently the place appealed to the young execs as well as the pink-hairs.

She grabbed a table and said, "You'll have to go to the bar to get the drinks. I'll take a beer. Michelob."

I took the beers back to the table, sat down, and slid hers across the wooden table.

"What about Jodi? Is she in trouble?"

"As a matter of fact, she is. It has to do with a missing art object."

"You mean she did it?" Her skin was a light brown, but her eyes were like dark chocolate.

"Did it?"

"Hocked one of her stepfather's pieces."

"Oh yeah, she did it, all right. Now I'm trying to help her get it back."

"How can I help?"

"You introduced her to Terry Jacks, didn't you?"

"Terry? Why, yes, I did. What does he have to do with this?"

"I'm just interested in anyone Jodi met this month, Miss Jackson—can I call you Janet?"

"I don't even know if I should be talking to you, at all," she replied warily. "How do I know you're really working for Jodi?"

"You could call her."

"Is she home?"

"No, she's at a number I can give you."

143

"That doesn't sound right. How do I know what number you're giving me?"

"You'll recognize her voice, won't you?"

"Of course."

I took out a pen and wrote down Sam's phone number on a napkin.

"Here. Give her a call and ask her if you should talk to me."

She took the napkin but hesitated, studying me.

"I'll even give you the quarter for the call," I said, handing the coin over.

She smiled and took the quarter, making me feel as if I'd won a small victory.

"There's a pay phone in the back. Wait here."

For a moment I thought maybe she was going to run out on me, but I was able to follow her progress to the back of the place and watch her talking on the phone. The conversation didn't take long, and in a moment she was walking back to the table, a whole line of guys turning their heads and watching her from behind. The view from the front wasn't so bad, either. She was wearing jeans and a pink bodysuit, and her nipples were clearly visible.

"Sorry I was so suspicious," she said, sitting down across from me again. "I don't like talking to cops, and a private detective is sort of a cop . . . isn't he?"

"I used to be a cop," I said. "I guess the smell is hard to shake."

"Jodi says you're okay, so go ahead and ask your questions—and you can call me Janet."

"Janet, I just want to know what you can tell me about Terry Jacks."

She shrugged and said, "He comes into the store to buy records. That's how we met. He asked me out, we went out a few times, and that was that."

144

"When did you introduce him to Jodi?"

"At a party that I gave. I invited them both, not particularly to introduce them, but it seemed like a good idea at the time."

"Did you talk to him about her afterward?"

"He came into the store once or twice, but we never discussed Jodi."

"What about Jodi? Did you talk with her about him?"

"Just girl talk, you know?"

"Girl talk."

"Have you ever talked to a guy about a girl he went out with?"

"I think I know what you mean."

"What can you tell me about him personally?"

"He's good-looking, he likes girls very much, all sizes and shapes—and colors." She graced me with an infectious grin. "You like girls in all colors?"

I grinned back and said, "*All* colors. What else about Jacks?"

"Um, he's got money, he's blonde, fair-skinned, he's fairly good in bed"—she said this last while studying me with raised eyebrows; I didn't rise to the bait—"and he's got a bad temper."

That interested me.

"How bad?"

She hesitated, then said, "I'm only telling you this because you're a friend of Jodi's."

"Okay."

"After we went out a few times, he got rough with me one night."

"Did he hit you?"

"Once, and I kicked him out."

"But you invited him to your parties?"

She shrugged.

145

"Most of the time he was a nice guy; I just didn't get my kicks the way he got his."

"Did you tell Jodi about this?"

"No. Maybe it was what he wanted to do just with me. I didn't want to . . . start rumors, you know?"

"I know."

"There's something else I never told her, too."

"What's that?"

"Terry's a switch-hitter."

"You mean, he's bisexual?"

"Yes."

"Are you sure?"

She grimaced and said, "Yeah. Some of my parties get out of hand, you know. I went to use the bathroom at my last one, and Terry was in there in the shower stall. He was getting some action . . . from a guy!"

"I guess you're sure, then. How long have you known Terry?"

"A couple of months. Ever since he first hit town."

"Where did he hit town from?"

She shrugged and said, "Who knows?"

It might have helped if I did. I made a mental note to remember to ask Jodi.

She hitched up closer to the table and gave me a different kind of look.

"Are you and Jodi . . . close?"

"I'm just trying to help her."

The bodysuit she was wearing was not particularly low-cut, but it had a rounded neck, and I was able to see the swollen beginning of her deep cleavage. That, combined with the fact that her nipples showed through the thin fabric of the top, made it impossible not to stare. She *saw* me staring and smiled.

146

"You're kind of cute, you know?" she said. "Why don't you give me your telephone number, and I'll invite you to my next party?"

It was a hell of a tempting offer, but her parties didn't sound as if I would fit in.

I smiled back and said, "I'm afraid I'm not exactly the party type, Janet."

"Well, then, come into the store sometime and buy some records. I'll make you a real good deal."

"I may take you up on that. You want to finish that beer?" I asked, indicating her beer bottle. It was still half full.

"I don't *have* to," she said, pushing her beer away. I left half of mine, also.

We stood up and started for the door, and I put one hand on her rounded shoulder as we reached it.

"Janet, would you do me a favor?"

"Sure, name it."

"Would you mind not calling Terry Jacks to tell him I'm coming to see him?"

She smiled and said, "Don't worry, Nick. We're not that close."

23

I had three choices on how to get uptown. I could walk, and since it was summer that would be a pleasure. On this day, however, I didn't feel like walking from Eighth Street to Eighty-third.

There was the subway, but I've explained how I feel about that.

The third choice was to take a cab, which would get me there the quickest and the safest—safe except for my wallet, of course.

The block and building that Terry Jacks lived in was in sharp contrast to Janet Jackson's. Eighty-third and York was high-priced, and if Jacks's father kept him on an allowance, it was a big one.

The doorman had to call upstairs to get the okay to send me up.

"What shall I say is the nature of your business?"

It never fails to amaze me how putting a uniform on a man whose only job is to hold the door open for you makes him think he's hot shit. This one stared down his nose at me in such a way that he might have simply been examining the tip of it for pimples.

"Tell him the nature of my business is girls."

I figured if he was as much of a pussy hound as Janet intimated, that should get his attention.

"Girls?"

"Yes, girls."

He looked at me, and then some of his icy facade fell away and he said, "That'll do it."

He called upstairs out of earshot, spoke briefly, then hung up.

"You can go up. Six-fifteen."

I took the elevator to the sixth floor, found 615, and knocked.

The man who answered the door was easily recognizable as Terry Jacks. He had blonde hair that fell to his shoulders. He was tall and slender, fair-skinned, and would probably be attractive to some women. Well, a lot of women.

"Terry Jacks?"

"Mr. Delvecchio?"

"That's right."

"Come on in."

He backed up and I entered, passing him. He closed the door behind us.

We were in the living room, which, for an apartment as expensive as this one, was rather sparsely furnished.

It was empty.

Oh, there were canvases and easels, some of them obviously works in progress, and drop cloths on the floor, but other than all of that and a stereo with miniature speakers, the room was bare.

"I live simply," he said, by way of explanation. "My supplies, my stereo, and my bed—speaking of which, you said something about girls?"

He wore an open, good-natured expression.

"One girl in particular."

"Which one is that?"

"Jodi Hayworth."

"Jodi—yeah, I know Jodi. You a friend of hers?"

"Sort of."

He frowned, the good-natured expression slipping slightly.

"What does 'sort of' mean?"

"I'm working for her."

"As what?"

"I'm a private investigator."

Now his expression turned wary.

"A private eye? Why would Jodi need a private eye?"

"There's a piece of artwork missing from her house."

"And she thinks I took it?"

"No."

"Then why are you here?"

"Just to talk to you."

"Well, I'm pretty busy—"

"It won't take long."

"Look," he said, "I can't help you. I don't know anything about artwork—"

"Sure you do. You're an artist. You know when a piece of art is worth money."

"So? That doesn't mean I took something from her house. I've only been there once or twice."

"What did you think of her stepfather's collection of art?"

"He's not much of a collector, just some small statues and busts."

"I thought you didn't know anything about art?"

"Like you said, I'm an artist, but I don't know anything about any missing art pieces."

"I never said you did, Terry."

"Then what are you doing here?"

"Let me tell you about detective work, Terry," I said. Calling him by his first name was something they taught you in the academy. Investigators use it to intimidate witnesses and suspects. "All it is is asking questions, some of which don't make any sense."

"Well if that's the case, then you must be doing it right."

I couldn't argue that.

"This place must cost you plenty. You must be doing pretty well with your paintings."

"I've sold one or two."

I walked over to a couple of the canvases, but he quickly moved in front of me.

"I don't like people to look at my work before it's done."

I couldn't blame him for that, either. From what I could see, he was a pretty piss-poor painter.

"Listen, I'm really busy. I'm being honest with you, I don't know anything about a piece of art missing from Jodi's house."

"She says she remembered you picking up a piece or two to examine."

"All right, that's enough," he said, getting angry. "I'd like you to leave before I call the doorman and have him throw you out."

"Do doormen do that?"

He grinned tightly and said, "They do if they want their Christmas envelopes."

"What's your father's name?"

"What's that got to do with anything?"

I shrugged.

"Just one of those questions that doesn't seem to make any sense."

"I'm calling the doorman."

He walked over to a telephone on the floor and picked up the receiver. Seeing him with it made me think back to that first night, when I'd gotten the call warning me to keep away from the "hole thing."

"It's okay, Terry, I'm leaving."

He stopped and stared at me, still holding on to the receiver.

"I might want to talk to you again, though."

When he replied, I listened real close, trying to imagine his voice coming over a phone.

"If you do, you better have a better reason next time, or you won't get past the doorman."

"I'll remember that."

I let myself out, and in the elevator on the way down I thought about what I'd told him about questions that didn't appear to make any sense.

This case was full of them, starting from day one.

Who had called me on the phone, warning me off a case I wasn't even on yet? Had it been Terry Jacks? Or Jodi's captor, Carmine DiVolo? Or somebody else I wasn't even aware of yet?

What was so goddamned important about a doughnut-shaped piece of art?

Why was I worried about this shit when my sister's life was in danger?

Why hadn't I given foxy Janet Jackson my phone number?

24

I got to Bogie's after four o'clock and found Miles Jacoby waiting for me there. He was sitting at the bar with a bottle of St. Pauli Girl in front of him. Jack and I had met when a case took him to Brooklyn and he needed a P.I. who knew the lay of the land. I was recommended to him by another P.I. we both knew, Henry Po. We got along, and he uses me when he needs something done in Brooklyn, and I use him when I need something done in Manhattan.

Seated on a stool next to him was a man with a mustache so bushy that you couldn't see his upper lip. He was in his mid-thirties, a man of medium height who obviously kept himself physically fit. His name was Billy Palmer, and with his wife, Karen, he owned Bogie's.

Jacoby himself was in pretty good shape, but then he should have been. He was an ex-middleweight and had recently begun working out in karate. At thirty—several years younger than myself—I thought he might have his eye on a comeback of some kind, but meanwhile he had turned himself into a pretty good investigator for someone who had come to it late.

Bogie's bar was separated from the restaurant by a brick wall with two arches. Above the arches, all across the wall, were framed book covers and photos from mystery writers, all signed to Billy and Karen. In the three short years since they opened Bogie's, it had become a true haven for mystery writers, serving as the site for gatherings, awards presentations, and just plain dinner.

Jacoby saw me as soon as I entered and waved me over.

"Elias, get my friend a beer," he said to the bartender, a young, good-looking Hispanic.

The bartender looked at me, and I pointed to the bottle in front of Miles.

"The same."

"Nick, you remember Billy."

"Sure, how are you?"

"Fine," Billy said as we shook hands. "Can we get you some dinner while you're here? We've got a new chef who's a hell of a cook. My wife swears by him."

"How is Karen?"

"She's fine, working hard as usual."

His wife was a foxy brunette with more energy than half a dozen normal people.

"In deference to her chef, I have to get back to Brooklyn."

"Brooklyn," Billy said, shaking his head. "The great unknown."

"You've never been there?"

"Once or twice to a friend's house for a party, but we always took a cab. I'd never be able to find my way around by myself."

"Well, I'm not all that fond of Manhattan," I admitted. "For me there's no exit from Brooklyn. I was born there, and I can't imagine living anywhere else."

"Billy," Elias said as he put my beer down, "they want you in the kitchen."

"Excuse me."

Billy left, and I turned my attention to Jacoby.

"Let's get this over with. You've got to get back to Wall Street to follow Numbnuts home."

"Numbnuts?"

"My brother-in-law."

"Well, I don't know whether it's good news or bad news, but there's no need for me to have to follow Numbnuts home."

"There isn't?"

He shook his head.

"He's having it off with a clerk in his office."

"A clerk?"

"A sweet young thing with stars in her eyes, from the looks of it. They go to the Howard Johnson's on Fifty-first and Eighth."

"Howard Johnson's?"

"Your brother-in-law is not much of a high roller, but it apparently doesn't matter to the lady."

"Could this have been a one-time thing?"

"Not from the looks of it, Nick, but I can check it out again tomorrow if you like."

I stared at the green St. Pauli Girl bottle in my hand, which I was holding by the neck. I wished it was my brother-in-law's throat.

"Yeah, all right," I said. "Just find out if they make it again."

"I'll talk to the clerk at the Howard Johnson's and see what he can tell me."

"Fine."

I put the beer down on the bar, still staring at it.

"Say goodbye to Billy for me, will you?"

"Sure. How you holding up, buddy?" he asked, touching my arm.

"Okay, I guess. I'm trying to keep busy."

"Must be a bitch. Let me know if there's anything I can do to help . . ."

I looked at him and said, "Can you call me tomorrow evening?"

"Sure, no problem. I'll know something by then."

"Thanks, Jack, I appreciate this."

"I'm sorry it turned out this way, Nick. Your sister doesn't need this kind of trouble on top of everything else . . ."

"He's an asshole, anyway."

"Are you going to tell her?"

"She probably already knows, but I'll decide if—when she comes home."

I clapped him on the shoulder and said, "Thanks. See you."

"Take care."

I left Bogie's feeling even worse than before, if that was possible. I think I'd been secretly hoping my brother-in-law was clean and that my sister's and his problems were nothing more serious than socks being left on the floor, or burning his toast in the morning. Those things could be worked out between them.

Now that I knew he was cheating on her, I wished I didn't.

25

Returning to Brooklyn from Manhattan was always the source of great pleasure for me, however I chose to do it. What I had told Billy Palmer about there being no exit from it for me was true. There was no place else in the country—or the world, for that matter—I could ever have imagined living.

I wanted to get back as quickly as possible, so I grabbed a cab from the corner of Twenty-sixth and Seventh, right down the block from Bogie's.

When Sam opened the door of her apartment to my knock, there was a definite chill in the air.

"Sam—"

"Don't ask," Sam said quietly but firmly. "Just come in and get her."

I stepped in and saw Jodi sitting on Sam's couch. When she saw me, she grinned and stood up.

"You're back."

"Yeah."

"Can we . . . get out of here?"

I frowned, wondering what had gone on while I was away— and then I remembered the last words Sam had said to me that morning before I left.

What *had* they found to talk about that had turned the air so cold?

"Sure, Jodi. Come on. We have to talk."

"Fine." She brushed past Sam on the way out. "Thanks for the use of the hall," she said sarcastically.

She went past me then and out into the hall, where she waited in front of my door.

"Sam, what went on?"

"Remind me to tell you sometime," Sam said, her expression unreadable, then she added, "that is, if she doesn't first."

"I don't—"

"Just watch out for yourself with her, Nick. She's trouble."

Tell me about it, I thought. Already I'd been hauled in by the police and attacked by two bruisers because of my initial association with her, however brief it had been.

"Thanks for your help."

"Sure," she said, "but I don't think it would work again. All right?"

"Yeah, all right. Talk to you later."

I went out into the hall where Jodi was waiting and unlocked my door. When we got inside she whirled on me.

"What did she tell you?"

"Who? Janet?"

"No, your friend, Samantha."

158

"She didn't tell me anything, why?"

"Nothing. What happened with Janet?"

"I've got to make a call first before we talk. Could you make some coffee?"

"Sure."

While she went into the kitchen, I called Ed Gorman.

"Were you able to find out anything for me?"

"How much do you already know about this case, Nick?"

"Nothing."

He heaved a sigh on the other end that almost blew out my eardrum and then started talking.

"The victim is James Berry, male, white, fifty-four, shot in the chest at close range with a .32 caliber revolver, said weapon not recovered."

"Married?"

"No, lives alone."

"Job?"

"He's wealthy—or he was. He made investments from his home." I wondered what Mr. James Berry, who made investments from his home, had been doing down on Atlantic Avenue in a two-bit hockshop, but I couldn't say that to Gorman.

I waited, and when nothing further was forthcoming I said, "Suspects?"

Another sigh and then, "One."

"Ed, do I have to drag this out of you?"

"I get the feeling I'm walking a one-way street here, Nick. Are you sure you don't know anything about this case?"

"Nothing that would help Westchester find the guy's killer." That was as honest an answer as I could give him.

"All right, it gets a little funny here. A blonde girl was seen going into the house the day Berry was killed. Later she was seen coming out, and then three men grabbed her. One went into the house while the other two stayed outside with the girl.

159

When the first guy came out, they all got into a car and drove away."

"So the cops are looking for all of them?"

"Right."

"Have you got good descriptions of all four?"

"Yes. Sometimes it pays to have a nosy neighbor in the area."

He reeled off the descriptions. Jodi was easy to recognize, as were the two goons who had visited me. The fourth man I didn't know about, but I was sure Jodi would tell me the description fit DiVolo.

"But they're not looking for all four."

"Why not?"

"Delvecchio, you better be being straight with me on this."

"Ed—"

"Never mind. One of the men was found dead the other night."

"How'd that happen?"

"Who knows? He was found in a dumpster with a broken neck."

"A dumpster?"

"In a residential area of Marine Park. Some people rented one because they were tearing down their garage, but they came out one morning and found this guy in it. You want his name?"

"That'd be nice."

"Yeah, well, his name was Lester Wexler, and he had a yellow sheet as long as his arm—his *strong arm*."

"Who was he working for?"

"He was free-lance. Looks like he finally took one job too many."

"Ah, the tough life of a torpedo."

"God, I haven't heard that expression in years."

"That's what they called them in your day, isn't it?"

160

"Trying to keep me from asking any questions, aren't you? Like what your interest is in this murder?"

"I'm just . . . interested. Are these other three people being sought as suspects?"

"Officially, they're wanted for questioning. Only two of them were seen entering and leaving the house, so only two could be called suspects. One of the men and the blonde girl—who sounds just like your type, by the way."

"Not me," I said quickly, "I hate blondes."

"Uh-huh. Listen, Westchester is real interested in why I'm interested."

"What did you tell them?"

"I told them I had a tenuous interest, and would certainly let them know if I came up with anything to help them. That's right, isn't it?"

"That's exactly right, Ed. I couldn't have put it better myself."

"Uh-huh, you eloquent sonofabitch, you. How's your family doing?"

"Hanging in, Ed, thanks."

"I don't have any further news for you. Things seem to be at a standstill over there. The Lebanese government doesn't want to release any prisoners."

"Are they still on the plane?"

"Yeah, but that's subject to change, too."

I felt a chill, suddenly.

"What do you mean?"

"Well, they're asking for a bus."

"They want to take the hostages off the plane?"

"Yeah."

"They can't do that! If that happens, how will we know where they are?"

"We won't."

"Ed, has this been on the news?"

161

"Not this part of it, no, but they can't keep it from the press for very long. Try and let your father know so he doesn't hear it on T.V."

"Yeah. Thanks again, Ed."

"And do me a favor."

"What?"

"Don't get in over your head with this Westchester thing."

"I always manage to keep my head above water, Ed. You know that."

26

When I hung up on Gorman, Jodi came in with the coffee pot and two cups on a tray.

"News about the hostage situation?"

I looked at her.

"Samantha told me about it. I really appreciate your helping me with my problem, Nick, what with your sister . . . uh, you know . . ."

"I know. Don't worry about it. Let's talk about your problem."

"Which is?"

"The Westchester police are looking for you."

"Oh."

"That's the bad news."

"What's the good news?"

"They're looking for two men, as well."

"*Two* men? There were three."

"One of them has turned up . . . dead."

"DiVolo?"

"No, one of the others."

"How did that happen?"

I shrugged as casually as I could.

"They don't know. Somebody broke his neck."

"That makes two people dead, and all because of that hole thing."

"Three."

"What?"

"Three people are dead," I said, and told her about the old man in the hockshop, how he had been tortured for the Westchester address and then killed.

"Jesus, I can't believe this."

I'm afraid I had the hostage situation more in mind than hers when I said, "Yeah, neither can I."

We sat in silence for a moment, and then I shook myself off and addressed myself to the present.

"Jodi, this is the way it sits. The police are looking for a blonde girl and three men, all of whom were seen at that house in Westchester. A man and woman were seen going in and coming out. Anybody with one good eye would be able to match you to the description of the girl."

"And DiVolo to the man's description."

"Right."

"What did you find out from Janet and Terry?"

"Janet cooperated, but Terry was nervous. Do you know who his father is? He wouldn't tell me."

"No, he never told me, either."

"And he never paid an inordinate amount of attention to your stepfather's statues?"

"Not that I noticed."

I sipped my coffee and said, "I'd really like to find out who's paying his bills."

"I could ask him."

"No, I don't want you going near him, or anyone until I can figure this out."

"Ah, the jealous type."

I gave her a sidelong glance and said, "No, not particularly." I drank some more coffee, and then she poured me another cup.

"What happened with you and Sam?"

"Why?"

"I detected a chill in the air when I arrived."

"We didn't really get along."

"You want to leave it at that?"

She thought a moment and then said, "Sure, why not?"

"Fine. You want to get some dinner?"

"Definitely. Where should we go?"

"Nowhere. I've got some menus in the kitchen. We'll order out and have it delivered. Why don't you do the honors?"

"Sure. Where are they?"

"In the drawer next to the stove. Here, you can take this with you, too."

I gulped down some coffee and put the cup down so she could take the tray with her.

While she was in the kitchen studying menus, I went into my office and opened the safe in my floor. I took out the .38 I keep there, well oiled and as neglected as I could possibly make it. I could count on one hand the times I'd held it since leaving "the job." I took it out of the safe and stuck it in the

165

top drawer of my desk. I hoped it would stay there, but somehow I was more comfortable that it was more accessible.

"Is Italian all right?" she asked as I entered the kitchen.

She had the Italian restaurant menu spread out on the counter and was bent over it. She was wearing tight shorts that molded themselves perfectly to her shapely hips.

"Italian's fine."

"What's good?"

"The lasagna and the baked ziti are the best."

"Let's get one of each."

"Fine."

"And some pizza."

"Fine."

She stood up straight and looked at me.

"You're worried."

"Yes."

"About your sister."

"And about us."

"You don't have to go on with this, you know. It really is my problem. I could go to my stepfather—"

"Tony Macaroni."

"What?"

"I knew your stepfather a long time ago, Jodi."

"That's right, you said you knew him. Where was that?"

"A long time ago. I was just a kid, and he was a legbreaker on the docks where my father worked in Brooklyn."

"And they called him Tony Macaroni?"

"That's what they called him."

"I always thought of him as Tony Ronzoni, but I like Macaroni better. Wait a minute."

"What?"

"What's a legbreaker?"

"Just what it sounds like. Somebody who breaks your leg if you don't come across."

166

"With what?"

"Whatever," I said, shrugging. "If you work for a shylock, it's money."

"Who did Tony Macaroni work for?"

"He free-lanced," I said. "Why don't you call in that order, and then I'll give my brother a call."

"Your brother the priest?"

"You and Sam must have talked a lot, huh?"

"We did . . . but in the end we didn't get along." She picked up the menu and said, "I'll call this in."

After she called, she went to the bathroom, and I called Father Vinnie. He said that Pop was the same, still sitting in front of the T.V. I told Vinnie what Ed Gorman had told me, and he remained silent for a moment.

"You want me to tell Pop?" he finally asked.

"I'll come by in the morning and tell him, Vin."

"Nick—"

I could tell by his voice that something was wrong.

"What?"

"When you come—listen, Pop's been talking, you know how he gets—"

"What's he saying now?"

"He's been wondering where you are, why you're not with your family."

I rubbed my forehead, feeling a headache coming on.

"Yeah, well, I'll talk to him in the morning, Vinnie."

"He's just talking, Nick—"

"Yeah, yeah, I know how he gets. G'night, Father."

I hung up and sat down on the couch with my face in my hands. I didn't know Jodi was in the room until she put her hands on my shoulders.

I put my right hand over her left—which was on my left shoulder—and asked, "Do you have any money, Jodi?"

"Yeah, why?"

167

I patted her hand and said, "Because you're the client, and you're paying for dinner, kid."

She gave me a shot behind the head and said good-naturedly, "Bastard!"

It wasn't until she went to the bathroom again after we'd eaten that I realized that I'd missed something earlier.

When she came out, I said, "Let me have it, Jodi."

"Have what?"

"You know what. The coke."

"What coke?"

"Don't bullshit me!"

"You want to do some?" she asked. "Why didn't you say so?"

"I don't want to use it, honey, I want to lose it."

"You're kidding," she said, taking what looked like aluminum foil from her pocket. "This stuff costs money."

"It could also cost me my license if it's found in my apartment."

"Don't be like that—"

"Jodi, if you want my help, you'll give me the rest of that and stay straight until we've solved this thing."

"Nick—"

"Those are the only conditions under which I'll continue working for you."

She stared at me, and then at the wad of foil in her hand.

"Self-righteous bastard!" she said, tossing it at me. It bounced off my chest, and I picked it up. "You're so much better than I am, you and your girlfriend next door."

"Sam—"

"Your precious Sam. Why don't you just go next door and bang her tonight, because you're not getting any from me tonight, pal!"

"Sam and I don't have that kind of relationship."

"Oh, now who's bullshitting who, *Nicky?*" If my name had come out with any more sarcasm on it, it would have disintegrated.

"Jodi, we've got enough problems without getting into a fight."

"Fine! We won't fight," she agreed.

She walked over to my modest stereo setup and began looking through my albums.

"Jesus, don't you even have any decent records?"

I consider the small collection of records I have to be decent. Basically, I collect albums by artists who either were born or grew up in Brooklyn. They include Streisand, Neil Diamond, Neil Sedaka, and Billy Joel.

I mean, who doesn't like Billy Joel?

She was pushing me to see how far she could go, and when she realized I wasn't biting, she gave up.

"I'll take the damn couch, and you take the bed, and we'll go to sleep. We've got a big day tomorrow, right?"

"Hopefully."

We stared at each other for a few seconds, and then I said, "Good night, then."

I headed for the bedroom, and she called out, "Hey, Nick?"

"Yeah?"

Indicating the foil in my hand, she asked, "You, uh, you're not gonna flush that, are you?"

I hefted it in my hand and said, "You'll get it back . . . when our *business* is finished."

So the sleeping arrangements were the same as last night, but with one difference. This time she stayed on the couch.

It was just as well.

27

I woke up to the sound and smell of sizzling bacon. Dressing, I hoped that it meant the fight we'd had last night was behind us. If we were going to make any sense out of this mess, we were going to have to do it together.

I had hidden the coke in a rolled-up sock in one of my dresser drawers and was wondering if I was really going to return it to her or not. Actually, it *was* hers, and who was I to keep it from her once our business was over? I wasn't in the business of reforming cocaine users—or abusers.

When I entered the kitchen, she was scraping some bacon and eggs onto a plate and setting it on the table, where a

smaller plate of stacked toast, glasses of juice, and two cups of coffee were already waiting.

"Smells good," I said.

"It's a peace offering," she said, turning away from the stove to face me. She was wearing the same shorts and top she had on the day before, and I realized suddenly that she had no other clothes. "My way of saying I'm sorry I jumped in your face last night."

"That's okay."

"And I'm sorry about . . . the couch."

"*You* slept on the couch last night."

"I know," she said, "that's what I'm sorry about."

As we sat down to breakfast, I said, "We're going to have to get you some clothes today."

"Does that mean I get to leave here?"

"I could pick them up for you—"

"I'd prefer to do that myself. I usually have to try things on."

"All right," I said, "we'll see what we can work out. I need to go see my father first."

"Any news?"

"None good," I said, and dropped it. She had the good sense not to attempt to pursue the subject further.

After breakfast while she was washing the dishes—and she volunteered to do it—she asked, "Can I come to your father's with you?"

"No."

"Why not?"

"Because things haven't been going well between my family and me during this . . . crisis. We don't need an audience when we're . . . bickering."

"I'm used to family strife," she said, drying her hands on a towel.

"Speaking of which, do you want to go back home?"

"Nope."

"Why not?"

"I still don't trust my stepfather. He might be in contact with DiVolo."

"How about calling your mother?"

"Nick, we've gone through this before. I don't trust anybody," she said, and then added, "except you—and even that goes against the grain."

"Well," I said, "that's a start."

I promised to come back and take her shopping after I finished at my father's house.

As I pulled up in front of my father's house in a cab—a *Brooklyn* cab, not one of those crazy Manhattan hacks—I realized that I hadn't even thought about stopping for pastries.

When I entered the house, Vinnie looked up from where he was sitting on the couch. He was wearing his priest's collar, as he had been all along, and I wondered why he had to do that, wear the damn collar in the house all the time. Or did he just put it on when he knew I was coming?

"Vinnie."

"Good morning," he said, standing up. "No pastries today, huh? Well, I'm glad I already had breakfast. Still, you could have brought lunch."

It was only ten o'clock, but that was my brother the father's way of telling me he had expected me earlier.

"Where's Pop?"

"In front of the T.V."

"Jesus, can't we get him away from that thing?"

He gave me a look—the one they learn in the seminary in "Stern, Priestly Looks 101"—but I refrained from apologizing. He deserved it for the dig about lunch.

"Where do you want to put him?"

172

"I don't know. Jesus, we could give him something to do, I guess."

Stern look number two.

"He's got something to do."

"Yeah, sit around and feel sorry for himself."

"You don't think he's got a right to feel sorry for himself?"

"No, I don't," I snapped. "For Maria, maybe, but not for himself."

"Nick—"

"Vinnie, I don't want to fight with you. I've got something to tell you and Pop."

"About Maria?"

"Yeah. Come inside."

We went into my father's room together, and he was sitting in his leather recliner. There was an empty coffee cup lying on its side on the floor at his feet, and his eyes were riveted to the screen. They were showing the earliest pictures they had of the plane and the hijackers.

"Pop, how can you keep watching that stuff again and again?"

He looked up at me, and he looked as if he'd aged five or ten years since I last saw him. Shit, he looked like my grandfather instead of my father.

"Pop—"

"This television," my father said, "is my only connection to your sister, Nicky. You want to take that away from me?"

"Pop, this isn't doing you any good. You can't watch T.V. all day and all night."

"I want to know everything that's happening."

"Vinnie and I can keep you informed."

"Your brother maybe, but you haven't been around, Nicky. Where've you been while your sister has been in the hands of terrorists?"

"Pop, I've been working—"

"Working?" The disapproval was plain on his face and in his voice.

"Yeah, Pop, it was something I started . . . before all this happened."

"I don't understand you, Nick. I don't think I've ever understood you—"

I looked at Vinnie, but his face was blank, the way it had always been when Pop was bawling me out.

"Pop, a girl's life—my life—may depend on what I'm doing. I can't just stop—"

"What about your sister's life?" he snapped at me.

"I can't do anything about that!" I was shouting, and it came out before I could stop it.

"Your brother Joey—"

"Joey's dead, Pop."

This time my words were soft, but they had more impact. He looked stunned, as if it was the first time he was hearing that bit of news.

"Nick—" Vinnie said, grabbing for my arm, but I shook him off.

"Look, Pop, we went through all of this years ago, let's not dredge it up now. I've got some news about Maria."

"What news?"

"There's been some talk that the terrorists might take the hostages off the plane."

"But if they do that, how will they know where they are?" my father asked.

"Pop—"

"No, you're wrong, Nick," he said, shaking his head. "If you're gonna bring me that kind of news, then don't even come around."

"Pop—"

He turned away from me and fixed his eyes on the television again. He was dry-washing his hands in his lap, over and over

174

and over again, and finally clasped them so tightly together that the knuckles of his thick, red dockworker's hands turned white.

"Pop, you've got to face the truth—"

"Nick," Vinnie said, taking my arm. "Come on, let's go inside."

I allowed my brother to draw me into the living room, because talking to my father was like talking to a deaf man.

"Why'd you tell him that?" Vinnie demanded.

"Because I didn't want him to hear about it on television."

"No, I mean where did you get it from?"

"Inspector Gorman. He got it from a contact of his in the State Department."

"How does a cop have contacts in the State Department?" There was an unspoken "mere" in front of the word "cop," the way my brother said it. I've never been able to understand how or why a priest should have such a low opinion of cops.

"He wasn't always just a cop, Vinnie."

I don't know if that satisfied him, but he let the subject drop.

"What you said in there."

"About what?"

"About your life, and a girl's . . ."

"Vinnie, try to understand. I can't do anything about Maria, but maybe I can keep this girl alive."

"Yeah," Vinnie said. "Well, while you're keeping her alive, don't forget about yourself."

"Yeah, sure."

Moments like that were few and far between for us, and it was awkward.

"Have you heard from . . . from Peter?"

"No, he hasn't called. Have you seen him?"

"No, I haven't." Briefly I considered telling him what Ja-

175

coby had told me, but I decided against it. I'd handle that part myself.

"I'll call, Vinnie. Try and make Pop understand what might happen, all right? So he's not surprised by it?"

"I'll talk to him."

"And do me a favor, will you?"

"What?"

"When I come over tomorrow . . . lose the collar?"

28

I took Jodi over to Fulton Street, where we shopped in Abraham & Straus and then went over to the Albee Square Mall to eat in their food court.

Years ago Fulton Street—like Flatbush Avenue—was packed with shoppers every day of the week except Sunday. (That was back when stores actually closed on Sundays.) In addition to A & S there used to be a Korvettes there, a Mays, a McCrory's, and dozens of smaller shops. About five or six years ago they decided to close the street and make an open-air mall out of it, and then they opened the Albee Mall right on Fulton, which was a smaller, closed mall with shops and a food court.

Malls had given birth to the food court, and as a fast-food fiend I was all in favor of them. This one, on the second floor, had a chicken place, a hot-dog stand, Chinese food, Greek food, a McDonald's, a pizza place, a pretzel stand, and an ice-cream parlor.

Jodi waded her way through some chicken, Chinese, and pizza while I settled for chicken and fries. Afterward we tried the ice-cream place, where I had a simple cone while she had a banana-boat surprise.

During the course of the day much of the toughness left her, and she relaxed more. I believe she really had a good time with me, as I did with her—in spite of the fact that I was carrying all of the packages. She did her shopping with a credit card that she wielded like a double-edged sword, cutting a swath through large department store and small clothing shop alike. She said she'd left her oversized bag behind when she escaped from DiVolo, but she didn't keep her credit card in there, anyway.

Over the ice cream she said, "Thanks, Nick."

"For what?"

"For this. You could have taken me out, let me buy some jeans and a top, and dragged me back to your place."

"You're going to be cooped up some until this is over, Jodi," I said. "Don't let this fool you, but I did want to give you some time out."

"And now it's over?"

"I'm afraid so. I'll have to take you back and then get to work."

"What happened at your father's?"

The question surprised me, and I decided to answer her.

"My father blames me for not going over to Beirut and getting my sister back."

"But that's crazy!"

"I know it . . . but he's got to get mad at somebody, and I'm an easy target. It's always been easy for him to get mad at me."

"I know how that feels, but what about your brother?"

"How do you get mad and pop off at a priest? . . . We'd better get back."

"Are you going to leave me with Sam again?"

"I don't think so. I get the feeling you two will never be the best of friends."

"Well, we're both blondes."

"What's that got to do with it?"

She shrugged and said, "We just started off on the wrong foot, that's all."

"Well, I've got someplace else to take you, and we can go there from here."

As we stood up, I stopped suddenly, and she said, "What's the matter?"

"I just thought of something."

"What?"

"Where's your car?"

She even had to stop and think, but then she said what I had been afraid she was going to say.

"It's out in Westchester."

"Great," I said. "I guess I"ll be going out to Westchester, after all."

29

"Who lives here?" she asked.

We were in front of a three-story building at Eighth Street and Seventh Avenue in Park Slope, a better than decent neighborhood that was not only residential, but had a lot of doctors' offices in the area. In fact, Methodist Hospital was only a couple of blocks away.

"A friend of mine, a computer nut who goes by the name of Hacker."

"A guy?"

"A guy I trust, so don't be thinking that he'll make any moves on you just because you're in the same apartment. He rarely comes out of his computer room."

We went up to the door, and I rang Hacker's bell.

"Who?" his voice squawked from the box.

"Nick."

"Hey, Nicky D. Come on up!"

"I've got a lady with me, Hacker, so clean up."

"That would take a month," his tinny voice called back, "but I'll give it my best shot."

He buzzed the door open, and we went in.

While we were walking to the third floor, she asked, "Why do you call him Hacker?"

"It's some kind of a computer term that he can explain to you better than I can, but in addition to that he hates his real name."

"What is it?"

"Wild horses couldn't tear it out of me. He'd tap into an IRS computer and have me audited every year for the rest of my life."

When we got to the door, it was ajar. I knocked, and we walked right in.

"Jesus," Jodi said.

The apartment was a mass of literature: stacks and stacks of magazines, literally rows of them, and all of them computer magazines. Most of the stacks were six feet high or less, but every so often there was one that was floor to ceiling, and these were usually made up of smaller stacks that were tied together.

"This would be the living room, if you could see it," I said. "Kitchen's over there, bedroom there, and that's Hacker's room over there. He's got a daybed in there, so you'll be using the bedroom."

"You know this place pretty well, don't you?"

"We shared it for a while," I said. What I didn't tell her was that Hacker took me in after I had to leave the department, because I couldn't pay my rent. I lived with him for four months until I found the place on Sackett Street.

181

"I'll get him."

I put down Jodi's packages and walked to the door of his room to pound on it with the flat of my hand.

"Hacker! Come on, man, you've got company."

The door opened almost immediately, and Hacker stepped out. I knew that on the other side of the door was a collection of computer parts—pieces from different systems—that he had set up into one of the most elaborate computer systems privately owned.

"Hacker, this is Jodi."

"Hello."

"Hi."

Hacker was about my age, but he was what was commonly known when we were in school as a nerd. All that meant was that he was one of the smarter kids in school who always had something on his mind and consequently gave little thought to things like his appearance.

He was tall, dark-haired, sallow-skinned, and painfully thin. He wore dark-framed glasses and a quick, contagious smile. He was a sweetheart of a guy, and I loved him like a brother.

"What's up?"

"She needs a safe place to stay, Hack."

"My friend," he said to Jodi, pointing to me. "Every time a woman needs a 'safe' place to stay he brings her to me. Tell me, do I look that harmless?"

"You look like a pussycat."

"I like this girl, Nicky."

"I thought you would."

I turned to Jodi and said, "Do whatever Hacker tells you to do. You can trust him like you trust me."

"Ha!" Hacker said, but he tempered it with a wink in her direction.

"You keep your hands on your keyboard, Hacker."

"Can she cook?"

"She made me breakfast."

"Then you're most welcome, ma'am. I'm real tired of eating out of boxes and bags."

"I'll see what I can do."

Such was the degree of our friendship that I didn't have to do any explaining to Hacker.

"Walk me to the door," I said to Jodi.

At the door she said, "Nick, he looks like a nerd."

"He doesn't happen to think that's something he should apologize for, Jodi. He's a good guy, and he'd go to hell and back for a friend."

"How many friends does he have?"

"Me," I said, "and if you play your cards right, you."

"When will you be back?"

"Later today."

"And then we'll go back to your place?"

"I don't know, maybe we'll just all stay here. We'll talk about it later."

"You're going to Westchester?"

"Yes, and that reminds me. Give me the keys to your car."

She reached into her new jeans and handed them over.

"Hacker," I said over her shoulder, "I need your car."

"Treat it gentle," he said, tossing me his keys.

"Or it'll fall apart," I added. I looked at Jodi and said, "The man drives a '77 Grand Prix that's got a hundred thousand plus on it."

"If you treat her nice, she runs fine."

"I'll treat her so nice she won't want to come back to you. Do me a favor while I'm gone."

"Like what?"

"Entertain this young lady. Show her some of your little toys."

"Sure thing."

"See you later, Jodi."

When I left, Hacker was telling her he was going to show her a computer no bigger than her purse—if she'd had a purse.

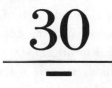

30

I took a lot of driving around, asking directions, and wrong turns, but I finally found Jodi's car parked down the block from James Berry's house. Actually, it was more than a house and just a little less than an estate. The grounds were enclosed by a black wrought-iron fence, and the house appeared to be two stories, with a Victorian slant to it. The front door still had a police department crime-scene seal on it.

I made a circuit of the block to see if anyone was watching Jodi's car, then parked Hacker's green Grand Prix a few hundred feet behind it because I didn't want the Prix and Jodi's sporty job seen together.

After leaving Hacker's house, I had driven to a pay phone

and made a call to a man named Plummer. Plummer is not a friend, but he is somebody I use to do odd jobs for me. Over the phone I gave him the address out in Westchester and told him to meet me there. The reason I needed Plummer was because I was one man and could not drive two cars.

I got out of the Grand Prix and walked back up to Jodi's car. I looked around, but there was no sign of Plummer, and it was then I got the idea of going into the house.

Or maybe I'd intended to all along.

Anyway, I found a likely stretch of fence that was covered by trees and made my climb. Happily, James Berry had not been paranoid enough to go in for an electrified model. When I dropped down to the other side, I waited to see what would happen—alarms, dogs, whatever—but apparently Mr. Berry hadn't had a paranoid bone in his body. When nothing did happen, I started moving.

I reached the house without incident and circled it carefully, looking for an easy way in. The best way appeared to be a pair of French doors. I peered inside and guessed that this was Berry's study. There was a desk which must have been where he was found.

I was wondering how I was going to get inside when the door I was leaning against swung inward. A quick look at the lock told me that I wasn't the only one wanting to get inside. Someone had been here ahead of me, picked the lock, and left the door open on their way out. Then I remembered what Jodi had said about breaking in, and wondered if this was her work.

There were two other possibilities.

One, somebody else—DiVolo, Terry Jacks, maybe Tony Macaroni himself, but *somebody*—had been there ahead of me looking for the art piece.

Two, the house had simply been burglarized, maybe by someone who watched the obits.

Whichever way it went, there didn't seem to be any good

reason to go inside and look around, but I was there, so I went in.

It occurred to me to safeguard my prints, but the place had already been dusted. I started with Berry's desk, the blotter of which had a very large bloodstain on it. I went through the drawers and found a lot of papers and reports which, if I had seen them earlier and had the money to invest initially, could have ended up making me a lot.

I was about to replace the folder I was holding when something jumped out at me through the closed cover. It was as if I had seen it, passed over it, and was suddenly seeing it again. I opened the folder again for a second look, and sure enough, the reports in this particular folder had been prepared by the investment firm of Fielding & Wilder.

That was the company my brother-in-law worked for on Wall Street.

Shit.

I replaced the folder and slowly closed the drawer. I moved out of the study to look through the rest of the house, pushing all thoughts of my brother-in-law to the back of my mind for the time being.

I checked drawers and cabinets, but it was obvious that they had been gone through before by somebody who knew what he was doing. Upstairs there were four bedrooms, but only one looked like it had been lived in. I went through Berry's dresser drawers and found nothing. Either anything to be found had already been found by someone else, or there *was* nothing to be found.

The house was filled with art: paintings, sculptures, several pieces to a room rather than all collected in one room. From what I could see, his pieces were far superior to what Tony Macaroni had in his house, but then I knew next to nothing about art.

I left the house, thinking about the deceased James Berry.

There was a possibility here that I didn't remember considering—but then my mind wasn't one hundred percent on this case. Whether I had thought about it before or not, I was thinking about it now.

What if James Berry's murder had nothing to do with Jodi's doughnut? True, the doughnut statue was not in the house, but Berry could have bought it and then sold it himself. He could have been killed for an entirely different, totally unconnected reason.

Which would really fuck things up.

I wondered if whoever did have the piece knew what they had, because I sure as hell didn't.

Outside, after retracing my steps, I found Plummer standing by the Grand Prix, which was the car I had described to him.

Plummer was forty-five or so, with thinning hair the color of a gray mouse and skin to match. He was an extremely unhealthy-looking individual, and would probably outlive me because he was also one of the luckiest people I knew.

"Plummer."

He whirled around, eyes wide, and then relaxed when he saw me. He was wearing jeans and a yellow T-shirt that said "Canal Hi Fi" on it. It also had some Chinese writing on it, which might have also said "Canal Hi Fi." I didn't know, and I didn't ask.

"Delvecchio, you scared the shit out of me, man." He tapped the hood of the Prix and asked, "Is this the rust bucket you want me to drive back to Brooklyn?"

"This is it," I said, handing him the key. "Treat it gentle. I promised the owner I would."

"Be gentle with it? The kindest thing to do would be to take it out and shoot it. Hey, I tried to get ahold of you the other day. Why don't you get a secretary, or an answering machine?"

"They both cost money. What did you want?"

"I had a good exacta for you."

"Did it come in?"

"Of course it came in. The top horse paid twenty, but the exacta only paid ninety. They're playing games out there, I'm telling you."

"Nothing we can do about it, Plum."

"Yeah, I know. Uh, by the way, what are you payin' me for this ride?"

"Walking-around money."

"Forty?"

"Twenty."

He looked like I had just scalded him with hot water, and screeched.

"That's all?"

"Look at it this way. You can put it on another exacta and turn it into nine hundred."

"Sure, sure. Can I get started? I been standing here for twenty minutes. It don't look good. Somebody's bound to call the cops."

"Look how far back from the street the houses are, Plum, and how much space is between them. How could someone see you standing here, unless they were looking for you?"

"I just get antsy being in one place for too long. Can I split?"

I had always suspected Plummer of having been a hippie in the Sixties, because every so often his speech pattern would fall into that time period.

"Yeah, okay, get going, Plum. Here's the address." I handed him a slip of paper with Hacker's address. "Just park the car as close to it as possible and leave the keys in the glove compartment." I reached into my shirt pocket and pulled out the twenty I had put there for him.

"Here's the twenty. Get going."

"You got it."

189

He got in the car, started it up, and peeled out, leaving some rubber behind. For a guy who didn't want to be noticed, he was a lousy driver.

I walked up the road to Jodi's car, climbed in, and fit the key into the ignition. I didn't turn it on because it was then that my brother-in-law's name finally came back to the forefront of my somewhat addled and confused brain. I hadn't wanted to stop and think about him while I was in the house. Shit, I never wanted to think about him, but I did now.

Fielding & Wilder was a big enough company, even though they were no E.F. Hutton. It shouldn't be any great surprise to find that a man of Berry's wealth was one of their clients.

The surprise had come at the top of one of the F & W statements, the box where it said, "Your Account Executive is"—and then it said, "Peter Geller."

Numbnuts.

31

So I used it as an excuse to go see him.

I drove to my sister's house in Bay Ridge, and used my key to get in. It was a key Maria had given me when she first got married, and Numbnuts didn't know anything about it.

When I got inside, something I'd often suspected about my brother-in-law was confirmed.

The man was a pig!

I mean, I'm not the world's greatest housekeeper myself, but this dude was the pits.

The kitchen was a mass of take-out cartons and bags, and filled-to-the-brim garbage bags. Out of respect for my sister, I cleaned up the mess while I waited for Peter to get home.

*   *   *

I was looking out the front window when he showed up, walking at a brisk pace. Today seemed to be a day that he came straight home from work, but then it was Friday. Who knew what plans he had for the evening.

Whatever they were, I was going to change them.

I saw him pause when he saw the pile of plastic garbage bags in front of the house. He looked at the house with a strange expression on his face, and it was then I realized that he thought Maria was home.

The man did' not look pleased.

He started up the walk slowly, and for a second I thought he was going to stop and turn around. I went to the front door and opened it, staring at him through the screen door.

"Come on in, Petey. We have a lot to talk about."

"What the hell—" he said.

I opened the screen door for him, and he came up the steps slowly.

"How the hell did you get in?"

Did I mention that my brother-in-law doesn't like me any more than I like him?

"I used my key."

He walked past me, then turned and said, "She gave you a key?"

"That's right."

"I expressly forbade her to give you a key." He said, "For Bad."

"Tough shit."

"What do you want?"

"I want to talk."

"I've got nothing to say to you."

He threw his briefcase on the couch and took off his jacket. He tossed it toward a chair and it missed, landing on the floor.

Every time I had ever seen him he was the very picture of

192

the successful young businessman: tall, about six-one, and physically fit. With his blonde hair, blue eyes, and fair skin, he didn't look at all Jewish. I always suspected that he bleached his hair.

It was his looks that first attracted my sister to him, but for the life of me I couldn't understand what hooked her beyond that.

"Do your clients know what a slob you really are?"

"Look, Nick, I'd like you to leave before I throw you out. You have no right here."

"Go ahead," I said, feeling like Clint Eastwood, "throw me out." Yeah, I almost said, "Make my day."

His muscles tensed, and I could see him considering it. My violent past may have had something to do with his decision to back off, but I'd like to think he was just a coward.

"Where've you been, Peter? You haven't been to see my father."

"Why should I go and see the old man? We hate each other."

"Out of respect."

"Respect," he said, making the word sound dirty.

"You don't seem all broken up about Maria being on that plane."

"There's nothing I can do about it."

"Sure there is," I said, "again in the name of respect. You could stop seeing your dollies."

"My what?"

On the way to the house I had stopped and called Jacoby at Bogie's. He said that the clerk at Howard Johnson's confirmed that my brother-in-law was there at least three times a week with his little girlfriend—and he said that she wasn't the first.

"Your girlfriend, Petey, the little girl in your office you fuck during lunch."

His eyes narrowed as he thought it over.

193

"Did Maria ask you to follow me?"

"She's in Beirut, you asshole."

"I mean before she left. Was it you—"

"I didn't know anything about it until yesterday. Did she know? Is that why she went away?"

"Why she left is our business, not yours."

"Wrong," I said, taking a step toward him. "I'm making it my business. If she dies over there, Peter, I want you to know that I hold you responsible, and I'll make your life a living hell."

"You—you can't threaten me."

"Open your eyes, fuckhead. I just did."

But he didn't give up that easy.

"You can't talk to me like I was one of your . . . your . . ."

"Scumbags. That's the word you're looking for, Peter, like one of the scumbags I deal with on the street, and you're wrong. I will talk to you like a scumbag because that's what you are to me. I've put up with your shit because of Maria, but Maria's not here now. You're not family, Peter, no matter what it says on your marriage certificate."

I took two more steps and planted a rigid forefinger right into his breastbone, hard! He flinched and took a backward step.

"I'm going to tell you a few things now, and you're going to listen. Number one, while my sister is in the hands of the terrorists, you're going to carry on like a worried, loving husband. You'll keep in touch with my father and brother, and you'll come straight home from work every night and stay home. Number two, you won't be spending any more lunch hours at Howard Johnson's—or at any hotel—banging little girl clerks. You got that?"

"I don't know who you think you are—"

I hit him a short one in the stomach, hard enough to drive

194

the air out of him. He doubled up, hugging himself, and I bent over so he could hear me real good.

"As far as you're concerned, motherfucker, I'm God. You'll do what I say, just as if I had passed some commandments down to you. You got that, scumbag?"

He glared at me through teary eyes and nodded. I decided to play on my violent history.

"I'd just as soon kill you as look at you, you bastard, but out of respect for my sister I'm going to leave you alive at least until she comes back. After that it's up to her."

I could tell by the way he was looking at me that he wasn't sure whether to believe me or not.

"Straighten up, now," I said, moving away from him. "I didn't hit you that hard."

He made a try at straightening, gasped, and then tried again and succeeded. He stood there rubbing his stomach.

"I always thought you were crazy, Nick, but now I know it."

"Careful," I said, wagging a finger at him, "you might make me mad. Do you understand all the conditions I just gave you?"

"Yeah, I understand. Now you can get the hell out of here."

"Speaking of here," I said, "when my sister comes home I want this house to be spotless. I don't care if you do it yourself or have somebody come in, but it better be done."

"Are you through playing tough guy?"

"Almost. Do you know a man named James Berry?"

"James Ber—what's he got to do with Maria?"

"Nothing. This is something else. Do you know him?"

"He's a client."

"He's also dead. What do you know about that?"

"Dead? What?" The look of confusion on his face could only be genuine.

"You don't read the papers?"

195

Looking dumbstruck, he shook his head.

"He was shot to death in his house. You wouldn't know anything about that, would you, Peter?"

"How would I know something like that?"

"Listen, haven't the cops been to see you?"

"No—the cops, why?"

"Well, there are financial reports on his desk with your name on them."

"My name?"

"I'm surprised they didn't see it, but then again, it could always be brought to their attention—"

"Nick, wait, I don't want to talk to the police—"

"Why not? Have you got something to hide?"

"No, of course not."

"Then why not?"

He was still rubbing his stomach, as if in a bid for sympathy. It was the wrong tack to take with the guy who had hit him in the first place.

"Well, you of all people should know that I don't like cops."

"Oh, really? And I thought it was just ex-cops named Delvecchio."

"No, look, see—"

"Nolooksee? Is that the way young upwardly mobile executives are talking these days?"

"Nick, let me finish—"

"You are finished, friend. I won't give the police your name if you'll do something for me."

His face brightened, and he even forgot about rubbing his stomach.

"What?"

"I want to know whatever you can find out about James Berry."

"Like what?"

"Like was he in financial trouble, was he seeing somebody's

196

wife, what was he into that might have got him killed? Oh, and did he collect art?"

"Well, he did collect art, I can tell you that. He haunted antique shops and hockshops, hoping to find something he could buy cheap and sell at a profit."

"That's the kind of stuff I want to know."

"Well—"

"But not now. Gather it up, and I'll give you a call. I'm hoping I won't need it, but if I do, I want to be able to reach you, so make sure you're always by a phone. Give me your business number."

He reached into his pocket, came out with a small gold case, and handed me one of his business cards.

"How many hot little numbers have you given this to?"

"None. I've never given out my home number."

"Sure, you're a real homebody."

"No, I'm not, but then neither is your sister."

"What?"

"Nothing . . ."

"No, no, never mind 'nothing.' You started to say something, now finish it."

"You'll hit me again."

"I won't."

He looked at me dubiously.

"I won't!" I insisted.

"Well . . . I wasn't the first one in this marriage to be unfaithful."

"What?" I asked, as if I hadn't heard him the first time.

"Your sister, Maria," he said carefully, "was fucking around first."

I hit him.

32

"You said you wouldn't hit me!"

He was sitting on the floor with a bloody mouth, and I couldn't hit him again unless I picked him up.

"Don't hit me again," he said as I hauled him to his feet.

"You're a liar, man!"

"I'm not!" he said. "Four months after we were married she was having an affair with a guy down the street. A month after that it was her aerobics instructor, and a month after that the mechanic who works on our car."

"And you stayed with her?"

He shrugged.

"The head of my firm likes to promote married account executives."

"Which is why you married Maria in the first place."

"Yes."

"And when she found out about it, she began having affairs."

"Well . . . yes."

"So it still all falls in your lap, shithead. We're back to square one." I pushed him away from me, and he staggered against a table. "The marriage is falling apart because it never should have happened."

He had the good sense to look embarrassed, and I hated to think that he might not be all bad.

"Look," I said, pointing a finger at him. "I'm not kidding, Peter. You stay clean until Maria gets back and we can clear this up."

"Do you think she's coming back?" His tone clearly implied that he didn't.

"She'll be back, and I don't want to hear different, understand?"

"Sure, sure . . ."

"Now you stay by a phone at all times until you hear from me."

"What about lunch?"

"Have it at your desk."

"I have meetings—"

"Leave a number where you can be reached—and if I find out it's a hotel—"

"It won't be a hotel," he said wearily.

He wiped a smear of blood away from his mouth with the back of his hand, then looked around for someplace to wipe that.

"I'm sorry I hit you the second time," I said, "but don't think I won't break your fucking head if—"

"There's no need for your garbage mouth," he said. "I understand."

I stared at him, wondering what would happen if anyone ever said "fuck" within the hallowed halls of the office he worked at.

"Okay, but remember this, too. If Maria doesn't come back, it's going to be the saddest day of your life—for all the wrong reasons."

He stared at me, then wiped his hand across his mouth again, nervously.

"Later, Pete."

I started for the door, then turned around and faced him again.

"Oh, one more thing."

"What?"

"I'd better not see your face on 'Good Morning America' or anything."

"How did you know—"

"I don't want you cashing in on my sister's situation, Peter. It would be a very bad idea to try and do that, believe me."

I left him standing in the middle of the living room looking at the blood on the back of his hand.

I walked to Jodi's car and climbed in. For the second time that day I was trying not to think about my brother-in-law, this time what he'd had to say about my sister.

I looked at myself in the rear-view mirror, slapped my own face, and said mockingly, "You garbage mouth, you."

It was getting late when I drove away from my sister's house and I had two choices: either go to my father's and call Jodi on the phone at Hacker's, or go to Hacker's and call my brother.

I decided to go to Hacker's. My father and brother might not have been happy at the moment, but they were quite safe from any sort of physical harm.

The same could not be said for Jodi Hayworth.

The set-to with my brother-in-law had only served to overburden my mind further. I could not quite reconcile myself to the picture he'd painted of my sister as the cheating wife. Oh, not that she wasn't attractive. There had been a time, however, where she had been an almost perfect Catholic. The first crack in that perfection had been marrying Peter Geller, and now, if my brother-in-law was to be believed, the second was adultery.

I hoped that wherever she was, she had not forgotten how to pray.

33

I found a parking spot for Jodi's car at one end of the block, then located Hacker's Grand Prix at the other end and removed the keys from the glove compartment. Then I walked to his house and rang his bell.

"Who is it?"

"It's Nick," I said into the intercom.

"Go away," Hacker said, "we're fornicating."

"That's okay, I only want to watch."

"In that case, come on up."

When I got to the third floor, the door was open, and cooking smells were wafting out into the hall.

"What's cooking?" I bellowed as I entered.

"Beef stew," Jodi shouted from Hacker's kitchen. "My own recipe."

I entered the kitchen and looked into the pot from over her shoulder. It looked delicious. The table was set with three places. There was a bowl of salad in the center, and a basket of Italian bread.

"Wait a minute," I said, knowing how well stocked Hacker kept his cupboard. "Where did all this stuff come from?"

"We went out and got it."

"I told you to stay inside."

"You told me," she said slowly, "to do what Hacker told me to do."

"And he told you to go out?"

"He told me to cook him a meal the likes of which he had never seen before, and that's what I'm doing. Besides, he went with me."

I stepped back and pretended to take a long look at her. She was wearing an apron that said "Computers Do It Better."

"Is this the tough little girl who came to see me a couple of weeks ago?"

"So I'm tough," she said, lifting her chin. "That doesn't mean I can't cook."

"Of course not. Where's the genius?"

"In his room. Tell him that dinner will be ready in five minutes."

"I'll tell him."

I went to the door of Hacker's room and knocked.

"That you, dear?" he called out.

"Yes, it's me."

"Come on in."

Every time I entered his room I felt privileged, because I knew he never let anyone else in there.

He was seated at an elaborate console, looking at a green screen with green print on it.

203

"How can you stare at that day after day and not go blind?"

"What?" he asked, turning to face me. He was doing something he used to do when we were in school together. He had rolled his eyes all the way up so that only the whites were showing.

"Very funny. Jodi says dinner will be ready in five minutes."

"She's a gem, that one."

"Why'd you take her out?"

"I was hungry."

"Hacker—"

"We only went to the corner, Nick, and nobody knows she's here, right? What's the harm—and smell that cooking!"

I inhaled and couldn't argue with that logic.

"Just don't do it again, huh?"

"Sure."

"We'd better go and eat."

"Nick—" he said, grabbing my arm.

"Yeah?"

"We haven't talked—I mean, about Maria . . ."

"We don't have to, Hack," I said, putting my hand on his arm. "We're friends. I know how you feel, so why embarrass both of us by trying to put it into words. You know how hopeless you are with words."

"Wait," he said. He turned to the console, cleared it, and punched up some keys. On the screen these words appeared: IF THERE IS ANYTHING I CAN DO TO HELP . . .

"I know, Wilbur," I said, "I know."

He hit another key and these words appeared: DON'T . . . CALL . . . ME . . . WILBUR!

"Nobody likes a wise guy, Wil—Hacker."

After dinner—enough of which we all consumed to stuff six normal people, and *still* there was some left over—Hacker

204

stood up and said, "I've got some work to do in my room now, and then I'll turn in. Jodi, that was a wonderful dinner, and I can't thank you enough."

"I'll put the rest away in the refrigerator for you, Hacker."

"What a good girl." He punched me on the arm and said, "Nicky D., you spending the night?"

"I don't think so, Hack. I'll see you in the morning. Make sure you lock your door, I don't want this lovely young lady to be tempted."

"If she only could . . ." he said, wistfully. "Good night."

After he left, I helped Jodi clear the table and put everything away.

"Are you leaving now?" she asked.

"After I make a call, which I should have made before we ate."

"Your father?"

"Yes."

"I wish there was something I could do to help, Nick . . ."

"You've got enough problems of your own to worry about, Jodi."

"Yeah, well, so do you, but you're taking time to help me with mine."

"It's my job."

"Sure."

I went to the kitchen wall phone and dialed my father's number.

"Vinnie—" I said when my brother answered, but he cut me off before I could say another word.

"Where the hell have you been, Nick? I've been calling everywhere!"

"Did something happen to Maria?"

"Not Maria," he said. "Pop."

"What's the matter with Pop?"

"He collapsed, Nick. He's at Maimonides Hospital."

34

Maimonides Hospital was on Fort Hamilton Parkway in the forties. I convinced Jodi to stay at Hacker's, and she convinced me to take her car. I had borrowed more cars during these past few days. . . .

Vinnie had gotten back there ahead of me, and I was surprised to see Sam there as well.

"What are you doing here?"

"Father Vincent called my apartment looking for you. When he told me what happened, I came right over."

"I'm glad you're here." I looked at Vinnie and asked, "What does the doctor say?"

"Pop'll be all right."

"What happened to him?"

"He's worn himself out, Nick, with worry, not keeping up his strength—"

"I thought you were seeing to it that he ate."

I hadn't meant it to sound like an accusation, but he responded as if it was.

"What do you expect me to do, force-feed him?"

"I didn't mean that—"

"Don't start arguing," Sam said, "not here in the hospital."

We both looked at her and then at each other.

"I didn't mean to accuse you."

"That's all right."

"Is Dr. Leary here?"

"Leary retired last year," Vinnie said. "Pop's doctor is Dr. Resner now."

"Resner? I don't know him."

"I recommended him to Pop. He's not Catholic, but he lives in my parish."

"When can Pop go home?"

"I've explained the situation to Dr. Resner, about Maria. He thinks we leave Pop here until the crisis is over so they can keep an eye on him."

"Good idea."

"Will your father go for that?" Sam asked.

Vinnie and I exchanged glances, and then I said, "He doesn't have to. We'll go for it."

"Here comes the doctor," Vinnie said.

Dr. Resner was a large man with a round, protruding belly that seemed as hard as a boulder, and a balding head. He appeared to be in his early forties.

"Doctor, this is my brother, Nicholas."

"Nice to meet you," Resner said, and we shook hands.

"How's my father, Doc?"

"He's resting. I've given him a sedative that will help him sleep tonight."

"Can I see him?"

"I don't think so. He's asleep already, and he needs his rest. Perhaps by tomorrow morning this terrible ordeal will be over."

"I doubt it," Vinnie said.

"Why?" I asked.

"Pop was watching television, Nick. It was when they announced that the hostages had been removed from the plane that he collapsed."

I kept quiet, not being the type to say "I told you so," but my brother could read my face pretty well.

"I see," the doctor said. "Well, I still think the best thing for him is to stay here where someone can keep an eye on him at all times."

"All right, Doctor," Vinnie said.

"He'll be yelling for a television in the morning," I said.

"Well, he'll have to pay to get one. Are you leaving him any money?"

"I haven't got any money, have you?" I asked Vinnie.

"Not a cent," my brother the father lied.

"Then he'll have to wait until one of you boys gets here and pays for it."

"Thank you, Doctor," Vinnie said, extending his hand.

"My pleasure, Father. I like your father very much and I'd like to help him through this."

"We appreciate it," I said.

He nodded, said good night to Sam, and walked away.

"Vinnie, where will you be?"

"I'll stay at the house, Nick, just in case we get some kind of call."

"All right. I'm going home."

208

"Can you give me a ride?" Sam asked. "I had to take a cab. Somebody forgot to fill my car with gas."

"Jesus, I'm sorry, Sam—"

"Never mind. Just give me a ride home."

"Sure."

We started for the front entrance, and then I froze.

"What is it?" Vinnie asked.

He looked where I was looking and saw the same thing I was seeing. Dominick Barracondi—Nicky Barracuda—walking in the front door . . . alone.

"Nick, Father Vincent. I came as soon as I heard." His tone was solicitous.

"Who called you?" I asked.

"I still have friends on your father's block, Nick."

That meant that somebody called him when they saw Pop being carted out to the ambulance.

"Pop's asleep, Mr. Barracondi," Vinnie said.

"That's all right, Father. I just want to talk to his doctor."

"About what?" I asked.

He looked at me and smiled, his teeth impossibly white for a man his age. They had to be capped.

"Your family has enough to worry about as it is, Nick, without having to be concerned with a hospital bill. I intend to take care of that."

"Is this another favor?" For a moment, as his eyes flashed and his smile slipped, I thought that maybe I had gone too far.

"This is something I want to do, Nick, for an old friend and his family. Allow me that privilege."

"Mr. Barracondi—" Vinnie started, but I cut him off.

"Whatever you say . . . Uncle Dominick."

He smiled without revealing his teeth, and for a moment he looked old, like one of the old men in the Italian club, drinking wine and reliving their pasts.

209

"Thank you, Nicholas."

He walked past us then, and I didn't know if he was thanking me for letting him foot the bill or for calling him Uncle.

Shit, I don't even know why I *did* call him that. Maybe I believed he was sincere in what he said.

He was still smooth, after all these years.

"What a charming man," Sam said. "Nick, was that really—"

"Yeah," I said, cutting her off and taking her by the arm, "that was my godfather."

We all walked out together, and then we walked Vinnie to his car before going to Jodi's.

"Nice car," Sam said, getting in. "Is it hers?"

"Yes."

"Is she at your place?"

"No, she's somewhere safe."

"And you? Are you going to stay somewhere safe?"

"I'm staying in my apartment."

"Well, that's smart." Needless to say, she was being sarcastic.

"If they come for me again, Sam, I'll be ready, this time."

"Good," she said, "maybe this time you'll kill both of them, or all three, or however many they send."

"I won't kill anyone, I'll just find out what the hell is going on."

"You still don't know? She hasn't told you?" "She" came out like a dirty word.

"What do you mean?"

"Just what I said, are you sure she's telling you the truth?"

"I think so."

"You think so."

I looked at her and saw that her jaw was firmly set.

"What's wrong?"

"You're letting that girl take you for a ride, Nick."

"What did she say to you?"

"Oh, nothing about the case. She just wanted to let me know in no uncertain terms that you were sleeping together."

"We're not . . . sleeping together."

"Oh? You didn't have sex with her?"

"Once," I said, and then immediately realized I'd made a mistake. I said, "Well, twice," and then realized saying that was a mistake, too.

"Well . . ." she said, and fell silent.

When we got to our building, we walked up to our floor. "Well" had been the last thing either one of us said.

"Sam, thanks for being at the hospital."

"Sure," she said, fishing in her bag for her key.

"About Jodi—"

"You don't have to explain anything to me, Nick. You're a big boy. I'm sure you can take care of yourself."

"Well . . ." I said, but she opened her door and went through, shutting it behind her without saying good night.

What was she so pissed at?

I unlocked my door, reached in and flicked on the light switch, and then went in quickly.

Empty.

I locked the door behind me, went into my office, and sat at my desk. I rubbed my face a couple of times with both hands, then took my gun out of the drawer and put it on top of the desk. It would be a good idea from now on if I kept it on me.

The last thing I remember before falling asleep at my desk was thinking that I had a holster in my desk somewhere.

35

It was morning, and somebody was trying to knock down the door to my office, which woke me—for which I was thankful. I'd been having a nightmare to end all nightmares, all about my sister and my father and Jodi and Sam and Hacker and a band of terrorists who were going to kill them if I didn't give them each a doughnut—and Father Vinnie wouldn't give me the money to buy doughnuts.

I sat up straight in my chair and caught myself reaching for my gun. I almost took it with me to the door, but some sixth sense told me to put it away in my desk. I opened a drawer other than the one it had been in before, and there was the holster that went with it. I fitted it into the holster, a clip-on belt type, and closed the drawer.

I went to the door and opened it. It occurred to me that if there was somebody on the other side who meant me harm, they wouldn't be knocking.

I was almost wrong.

"Matucci," I said, taking a step back. "What do you want?"

"Your ass, scumbag," he said. He moved into the room and his partner, Weinstock, came in behind him, looking embarrassed as always.

"I didn't know you went that way."

"I don't, dickhead, but you're going my way. Come on, let's go."

He reached for my arm, and I yanked it away from him.

"I just woke up, Matucci, and I haven't had my oatmeal yet. Can't this wait?"

"Murder don't wait, Delvecchio."

"Murder? Whose murder?"

Weinstock finally deigned to speak.

"We've received some information that you might be involved with a murder that went down in Westchester a couple of weeks ago. We'd like you to come with us to the precinct to answer a few questions, please."

"Now you see," I said to Matucci, "his mother taught him manners—but then, his mother also allowed him in the house."

"Cut the crap and let's go, Delvecchio."

Looking over Matucci's head—which pissed him off because it was so easy to do—I said to Weinstock, "Would you and your partner mind waiting for me in the hall while I freshen up? I answer questions a lot better when I'm not feeling so grungy."

213

"When is a private dick not grungy?" Matucci wanted to know.

"Private dick," I said to Weinstock. "He's been watching George Raft movies again."

"Come on, partner," Weinstock said, plucking Matucci's sleeve. "Let's wait in the hall while the man washes up."

"Sure," Matucci said, "and he goes out the other door."

"What's he gonna run for? All we want is to ask a few questions. So we'll watch the other door, too."

"Look, Weinstock—"

"Excuse me, fellas, but can you take this show on the road? I'll be right out, I promise."

"Don't fuck around!" Matucci said.

"Oh, no sir, detective, I wouldn't think of it."

They went out into the hall, and I closed the door behind them.

I had no intentions of trying to run away. Weinstock was right, all I had to do was answer their questions—that is, Lieutenant Wager's questions—and then I'd walk.

I went into the bathroom, removed my shirt, and started to wash up.

Of course, it didn't escape my notice that they had received a tip—and probably an anonymous one, at that—that I had some information about a murder in Westchester.

And who could have made such a call, I asked myself as I dried off.

Why, Numbnuts himself, my brother-in-law.

That asshole.

I got a fresh shirt out of my bedroom and slipped into it.

He was so reluctant to talk to the cops, what made him think that I wouldn't turn around and give the cops his name?

I mean, I wouldn't, but what made him think so?

That was easy.

He didn't know.

214

He'd simply made a dumb play that wasn't going to pan out—and when I finished with Wager, I'd let him know in no uncertain terms.

Feeling slightly less grungy, I went to my office door and opened it. I stepped into the hall next to Weinstock and asked, "Where's Matucci?"

Weinstock inclined his head to where Matucci was standing, further down the hall, in front of my apartment door.

"Oh you," I said, chastising him. "You just have no faith in anyone, do you?"

Looking disappointed that I hadn't tried to get away, giving him a chance to shoot me in the leg or someplace equally painful, he came slinking down the hall.

"Come on, come on . . ." he said, passing us.

I fixed Weinstock with a stern look and said, "Well, come on, come on!"

Wager was waiting impatiently in his cubicle.

"Sit down, Delvecchio."

"I want to commend these boys on their manner and class, Lieutenant," I said, taking a seat. "The little one there, the one who was too busy running his mouth to stand in line when God was giving out height, he didn't call me but three or four four-letter words all the way over here."

"Listen, you smart-mouthed fuck—" Matucci started.

"Ah, you ruined it!" I scolded him. Looking at Wager, I grinned and said, "That's five."

Wager fixed Matucci with a glare and said, "Get out."

"Yes sir."

Weinstock, ever the smart one, left with him without being told.

"What can I do for you, Lieutenant?"

"What do you know about a murder in Westchester?"

"I don't know anything about murder, Lieutenant."

"We got a call that said otherwise."

"Oh? And who called?"

"That's not for you to know."

"Oh, anonymous, huh? You guys putting credence in those kinds of calls now?"

Looking annoyed, Wager said, "We're just checking it out, giving Westchester a hand."

"Do they need one?"

"They're not getting very far—" he started to say, then seemed to realize who he was talking to. "Never mind. You sure you don't know anything about it?"

"If you'd fill me in on some details—"

"Never mind," he said. "I've got enough work of my own without filling you in on the details of a two-week-old murder case that wasn't mine to begin with. Go on, get your ass out of here."

"Sure," I said, getting up and heading for the door, "and you're welcome."

"For what?"

"I thought I heard you say something like . . . 'thanks for coming.'"

"Get out."

I shrugged and said, "Close enough."

36

I went back home, entered by the office door to be on the
safe side, and took a shower. Dripping, with a towel
around my waist, I called my brother-in-law's office.

He came on the line and said, "Geller."

"Hello, Numbnuts."

"Nick? W-where are you calling from?"

"Not from the slammer, if that's what you expected."

"Why would I—"

"Can the crap, Petey. You called the cops—my old precinct, too—and left an anonymous tip that I knew something
about a murder in Westchester. Lucky for both of us the message was taken by an incompetent and overworked lieutenant."

"Nick, I didn't—"

"You were so anxious that I not give your name to the cops yesterday, Petey, didn't it occur to you that I might throw you to them today?"

There was a long silent period, and then he said, "I didn't think . . ."

"Well, don't try. Just sit tight by a phone and wait for me to call you—and get to work on what I told you."

"All right, Nick, all right."

"Pop's in the hospital," I said before I hung up. "Maimonides. Send him a card."

"All right."

"Make it a Hallmark."

"Yes."

"A big one."

"All right."

I hung up on the obliging bastard, went into the bathroom, and sat on the commode, drying my hair. My next move was not crystal clear. Somebody had that doughnut, and somebody else—DiVolo or somebody he was working for—wanted it.

The big question for me was not who had it, or who wanted it, but why?

There was only one person who could tell me that.

I still had Jodi's car, but I couldn't use it to get where I was going, so I took a car service. I had the driver stop a few doors away from Jodi's house and wait and then walked the remainder of the way.

Jodi's mother answered the door.

"Oh, Mr. Delvecchio. Have you found my daughter?"

"Not yet, Mrs. Ponzoni. I have some more questions, however, which may help me. Is your husband home?"

"Uh, no, he isn't. Is there something I can do?"

"Possibly. May I come in?"

"Please."

She stepped aside, allowed me to enter, and then closed the door.

"Shall we talk in the living room?"

"Why not?"

On the way she asked, "Can I offer you a drink?"

"I don't think so. I won't be here very long."

"Well then, what was it you wanted to ask my husband?"

"I had some questions about the art pieces you and he own."

"He owns them, really. He had a small collection when we were married that he's continued to build up."

"Are they valuable?"

"Not really. It's more of a hobby than an investment."

"What about the missing piece?"

"What about it?"

"Is it valuable?"

"It is to him."

"Then why does he want it back so badly?"

"Mr. Delvecchio, do you collect anything?"

I thought briefly of my record albums by Brooklyn singers, but said, "No, not really."

"Then you don't know what it feels like to have a part of a collection missing. You want very much to get it back."

"I don't know that I understand him wanting the object back more than he wants your daughter."

"Well, she is *my* daughter and not his."

"I see."

It didn't seem to bother her that Ponzoni didn't want Jodi back. It obviously was not news to her.

"I guess that's it, unless your husband is coming back soon?"

"Not very soon, I'm afraid. In fact, I don't know when he'll be back."

219

"Has he gone out of town?"

"No, nothing like that, but sometimes his business keeps him out until all hours."

"I see," I said again. "Well then, I'll be going."

On the way to the door she said, "I'm sorry I couldn't be of more help to you."

"That's all right. I'll try to get your husband another time."

She let me out and closed the door behind me immediately. It's been my experience that when you let someone out of your house, you watch them walk away, just out of habit. That she didn't do this made me stop and think.

When I got back in my waiting car, the driver said, "Where to, pal?"

"Nowhere, for the moment. Let's just wait a few minutes and see what happens."

"You ain't a cop, are you?"

He was a middle-aged Hispanic with a wart on his left cheek and not much of an accent. His hack license on the seat back in front of me said that he was Fernando Velasquez.

"No."

"But in a few minutes, if somebody comes out of that house, you gonna tell me to 'follow that car.' Right?"

"Right."

"I was afraid of that. You a private eye?"

"Yeah, I'm a private eye."

"I'm keeping the meter running."

Since he was a private-car-service driver, he had no meter in his car, but I understood what he was saying.

"I wouldn't have it any other way, Fernando."

37

"She's heading for Staten Island."

"How do you know?" I asked him.

We were on the Belt Parkway moving toward Manhattan, which of course meant we were also heading for the Verrazano-Narrows Bridge, but right now it was a toss-up as to which borough she was going for.

"Educated guess," the driver said. "She your girlfriend?"

"My girlfriend's mother."

"And you followin' her to see if she's gettin' a little onna side, right?"

"Right."

"Well, if she's gettin' a little, my bet is she's headin' for Staten Island."

"Care to speculate a little further?"

"Sure. There's a Holiday Inn on Richmond Avenue. I've taken plenty of, uh, newlyweds there."

"Care to make a wager?"

"Sure. What's the bet?"

"Whatever I owe you."

"Double or nothin'?"

"Yep."

"You're on."

That was just to add some spice to the ride.

She hadn't wasted any time after I left.

She came walking down the front walk twenty minutes later and got into a small car with a Mercedes emblem.

"I know," my driver had said, "follow that car," and we had.

She had gone first to a ladies' lingerie shop on Eighteenth Avenue, one that specialized in sexy lingerie, and then had jumped on the Belt Parkway. Her choice of stores was what made me first think that she was—as Fernando also put it— steppin' out.

As we approached the entrance to the bridge and the Fourth Avenue exit, she moved into the right lane. She was either getting on the bridge to go to Staten Island or getting off at Fourth Avenue to go home.

When the time came, she got on the bridge.

"You lose."

"I thought the bet was the Holiday Inn."

"Geez, mister—"

"Not so sure now, huh, Fernando?"

Now it was his turn to add a little spice to the ride.

"Ah, what the fuck. You're on!"

We went over the bridge onto the Staten Island Expressway,

past the exit for Hylan Boulevard, which has its share of motels and inns. This reinforced Fernando's theory about the Holiday Inn—unless she was going to Jersey.

"Jersey," I said.

"What?"

"Maybe she's going to Jersey."

"If she's screwin' around, she ain't goin' to Jersey, pal. She woulda gone to the Golden Gate Inn in Brooklyn, or she's headin' for the Holiday Inn. Now from Manhattan, when they step out, they go to Jersey, but not from Brooklyn."

He sounded like the voice of years of experience.

"Where do they go when they step out from Long Island, Fernando?" I asked, just out of curiosity.

"Those people are crazy, man," he said, shaking his head. "They do it in their own *houses*. Don't shit where you live, that's my motto."

"And a good motto it is, too."

"See," he said suddenly, "she's gettin' off at Richmond Avenue. See the Holiday Inn?"

"Big as life."

We got off the exit right behind her, circled around, and came out heading south on Richmond Avenue.

"And there she goes," Fernando said, pulling over to the curb underneath the overpass. "Momma is definitely fuckin' around."

Mrs. Ponzoni had turned on her left signal, waited for traffic to allow it, and then turned left into the Holiday Inn parking lot.

"You win, Fernando."

We settled up, and then he said, "Want me to wait?"

I thought about it for a moment, then decided against it. If she was there to have it off with someone, then she would be inside for a while.

I didn't think I could afford Fernando's prices.

223

                              *   *   *

I crossed the street after the car pulled away and then ran over
to the hotel. I entered the lobby, shivering as a blast of cold
air-conditioning struck my moist arms.

Diane Ponzoni was standing at the counter, checking in. I
stepped off to one side and tried to be inconspicuous.

The clerk was all smiles and never even asked her if she
had any luggage.

That would have been the tip-off even if she hadn't paid him
in advance.

She'd been there before.

I wondered if the object of her affections was already there,
and then chided myself.

Grow up, Delvecchio. If the male half of this tandem was
already there, she wouldn't have to be checking in.

After she had taken her keys and walked quickly into an
elevator, I strolled up to the counter slowly, taking the time to
watch the floor indicator. It stopped at four, and then started
back down.

"Good afternoon, sir," the desk clerk greeted me cheerily.
Sure, I'd be cheery too if I had a fresh new twenty in my
pocket.

"Has Mr. Ben Franklin checked in yet?"

"Sir?"

"Yeah, I know, he gets kidded about it all the time. Has he
checked in?"

"Franklin. I'll check, sir."

He did his checking in his computer and then came back to
me shaking his head.

"I'm sorry, sir, but we have no Ben Franklin registered."

"That's okay. I'll just sit and wait for him."

"Of course, sir."

I sat in one of the lobby chairs with my back to the wall.
Somebody walking in would have to look way to his left to see

me, which wasn't likely since the front desk would be ahead of them and to their right.

It only took fifteen minutes for somebody I knew to arrive, and since I was a firm disbeliever in coincidence, he had to be there to meet Diane Ponzoni. Feeling surprised and confused, I watched him as he walked straight to the elevator, waited for it with his back to me, and then got in. He might have seen me just before the doors closed, but appeared to have something else on his mind. I watched the floor indicator stop at four—which was really pushing coincidence—and then the car started back down.

I sat there, wondering what my next move should be—that is, besides wondering what Diane Ponzoni was doing having an afternoon rendezvous in Staten Island with Terry Jacks.

38

I took the bus back to Brooklyn, figuring the ride would give me time to think. But things were no clearer when I finally arrived at home.

I spent the bus ride trying to figure out the connection between Terry Jacks, Jodi Hayworth, and Diane Ponzoni. Janet Jackson had introduced Jodi to Terry. Had Diane met him through Jodi, or did she meet him before her daughter did?

And what was Terry Jacks's game in seeing both? Was he turned on by screwing a mother and daughter without one or the other knowing about it? Or did he have something else in mind?

When I entered my apartment, I found a bottle of Dos Equis

in the fridge and took it into my office. At my desk I took out a lined yellow pad and began to make a list, using all capital letters, as if that would somehow make what I wrote easier to understand.

1. JODI HOCKS THE "HOLE THING."
2. THE OLD MAN AT THE HOCKSHOP SELLS IT, PRESUMABLY TO JAMES BERRY.
3. JODI HIRES ME TO GET IT BACK.
4. SHE SETTLES FOR THE ADDRESS OF THE MAN WHO BOUGHT IT, AND DISAPPEARS.
5. I'M VISITED BY TWO LEGBREAKERS LOOKING FOR JODI.
6. JODI SHOWS UP AT MY APARTMENT AND TELLS ME ABOUT JAMES BERRY'S MURDER.
7. THIS DAMN LIST IS TOO LONG.

I tore off the sheet of paper and started anew, listing only the most pertinent facts.

1. THE "HOLE THING" IS MISSING.
2. PONZONI WANTS IT, AND SO DOES DIVOLO, WHO IS SUPPOSED TO BE WORKING FOR TONY MACARONI. WHO IS DIVOLO WORKING FOR?
3. SOMEBODY HAS IT, AND PROBABLY KILLED JAMES BERRY TO GET IT.
4. TONY MACARONI PONZONI AND DIVOLO WOULD BE SUSPECTS, BUT SEE # 2.
5. TERRY JACKS—

I put the pen down abruptly. Obviously most of the questions that needed answering had to do with Terry Jacks, so he deserved his own list.

I started a new page.

1. TERRY JACKS WAS SEEING JODI, AND HAD BEEN TO HER HOUSE.
2. TERRY JACKS IS SCREWING DIANE PONZONI. (WHERE DID THEY MEET? AT THE HOUSE?)
3. TERRY JACKS IS A SUSPECT—BUT WHY WOULD HE WANT THE STATUE, AND WHAT'S HE DONE WITH IT? IF HE STILL HAS IT, WHY WAS HE STILL HANGING AROUND? WHAT ELSE COULD HE BE PLANNING?
4. WHO IS TERRY JACKS?

I put the pen down again. Terry's page was turning into an essay. I went back to the second list and added a question.

6. WHAT IS IT ABOUT THE STATUE THAT MAKES EVERYONE WANT IT?

I got up from my desk, walked around it, then stopped and leaned over to grab the pad again. I wrote one more question down.

7. WHO CALLED ME THAT FIRST NIGHT AND WARNED ME OFF—BEFORE I HAD EVEN MET JODI HAYWORTH?

I took all three pages into my apartment with me and sat on the couch. I spread them out on the coffee table and read them all.

Question number seven from the second list could very easily have gone to the head of the first list, because as far as my involvement went, it had happened before anything else. I tore it off the bottom of list number two and put it at the top of list number one.

When I was in Terry Jacks's apartment, I hadn't been able

to determine whether his voice was the one on the phone. It could have been him, disguising his voice. Or it could have been Carmine DiVolo, whose voice I had never heard.

If it had been Tony Macaroni disguising *his* voice, then that would mean he remembered me, and he had given no indication of that at his house. I was willing to disregard him as the man who had warned me off.

That left DiVolo and Terry Jacks.

I didn't think DiVolo was the man who had killed James Berry. For one thing he was still looking for the statue, and for another he wouldn't have had to go into the house after he grabbed Jodi.

I was willing to disregard him as the killer.

That left Terry Jacks—or someone totally unrelated to the statue.

I pulled the phone from the end table onto the coffee table and started making calls.

39

First I called my brother to see how Pop was. Vinnie wasn't home, so I assumed he was at the hospital. I knew I'd have to go over there later.

Next I called Jodi, at Hacker's apartment.

"Are you fornicating again?" I asked when Hacker answered.

"I've tried, but the girl won't have any. How's your dad?"

"Can't get Vinnie at home. I'll have to check in at the hospital later. What's Jodi up to?"

"She's cooking. I'll get her."

When she came on, she said, "Hi, how's your father?"

I told her the same thing I told Hacker.

"I need some information, Jodi."

"About what?"

"About Terry Jacks."

"What about him?"

"Where does he comes from?"

"He didn't tell me—"

"Think for a moment. Maybe he said something during a conversation that would give us a clue."

She took a moment and then said, "We only went out for a couple of weeks, a half a dozen times, maybe—wait a minute. I remember something."

"What?"

"He mentioned something about Cambridge once."

"Cambridge? In Boston?"

"I guess. He said something about Brooklyn reminding him of Cambridge, where he grew up."

"Boston," I said, half to myself. "I'll have him checked out."

"How?"

"I know somebody in Boston who can do it for me."

"What is it about Terry, Nick? Is he the one who killed Berry and took the hole thing?"

"The hole thing . . ." I repeated, this time low enough for her to be unsure that I was talking to her.

"What? What did you say?"

"Jodi, who else besides me knows that you call the thing a 'hole thing'?"

"I don't know—"

"Come on, think. Who'd you mention it to?"

"Well . . . Janet, when I told her I was going to hock it, and . . ."

"Terry?"

She was silent, and then she said, "Yes. Once when he was

231

at the house and he picked it up. He asked me what it was and I told him."

"All right!"

"What is it?"

"That night before we met, I got a call warning me off. The voice said 'forget the hole thing.' Who else would have referred to it that way? That's what you call it, nobody else."

"And I told Terry. So it was Terry who killed James Berry."

"That's a conclusion we can't jump to. All I feel I know now is that Terry called me and warned me off. Did you tell him you were going to hire me?"

"Yes. He called me and wanted me to go out with him, but I told him I had to meet with you."

"You specifically mentioned me by name?"

"No, I said I was seeing a private detective, and he asked me your name. I didn't think anything of it at the time, so I told him. But I told DiVolo that, too."

"Yes, but he never heard you refer to the statue as the hole thing. No, Terry called me." And Terry's sleeping with your mother, I added to myself. Did that mean she was involved?

"Jodi, did your mother—or Ponzoni—ever meet Terry?"

"No, I started going out with him while they were away."

Then how the hell had they met? I asked myself, not that it really mattered.

"All right. I've got some other calls to make. I'll talk to you later."

"All right—"

"Wait. One more thing."

"Yes?"

"Where in Greenpoint were you held? Do you remember the address?"

"Not exactly. It was on Franklin Avenue, near Greenpoint Avenue."

"Near the piers?"

232

"There were some piers there, yeah. I just kept walking away from the piers until I found a cab."

"Is there anything about the building that sticks in your mind?"

"Let me think. There was some writing . . . if I can only remember. . . . Wait, it said 'Imports,' that's why I remember, because Stepdaddy is in the import business. The writing said . . . 'J&D Imports.'"

"All right, good girl. Put Hacker back on."

"What's up?" he asked a moment later.

"I need you and your computer. Jodi will tell you everything she just told me. I'd like you to try and find out who owns the building."

"I can try," he said. "If I can't use the computer, I can always use the phone."

"All right. Give it your best shot. I'll call you back later."

I hung up and stared at my television set. With a start I realized that I hadn't thought about my sister all day. Would there be anything on the news about the hijacking?

No, I was actually better off not knowing, *not* thinking about her.

She'd be home soon.

I picked up the phone again.

40

I dialed Miles Jacoby's home number, hoping that he'd be there and not at Bogie's. I lucked out.

We went through the amenities about my father and sister, and then I asked him if he knew a P.I. in Boston. I knew he had a phone book that was filled just with phone numbers of P.I.s across the country. He'd inherited it from Eddie Waters, the man who taught him the business. Every once in a while he let me pirate a number from him, and I in turn put it in a book of my own.

He gave me the phone number of a man named John Francis Cuddy. Using Jacoby as a reference, I asked Cuddy if he could check up on a man named Terry Jacks, and gave him all the particulars. I even mentioned that he might have grown up in Cambridge. Cuddy said he'd be happy to run a check, and I asked him if he could do it as soon as possible.

After I hung up on Cuddy, I dialed my brother-in-law at home. He was there.

"What have you got for me on James Berry?" I said without preamble. What was I supposed to say? "How's it going, Numbnuts?" After all, I was turning the screws on my dear brother-in-law.

"I've made some notes . . . I'll get them . . ."

He sounded nervous, as if he was worried about pleasing me. I didn't feel sorry for the bastard.

He got his notes and started reading things off. A lot of them were inane and useless—he was left-handed, he liked soap operas, he had never been married—but then he said two things that interested me.

"He's gay, which somebody here told me. I never knew. Oh, and he collected art—"

"I knew that," I said, thinking of the things I'd seen in his house. Statues, paintings—

"He's gay, you said?"

"That's right."

"All right, Peter. Thanks."

"Does this help?"

"I'll let you know." I was not inclined to take him off the hook just yet.

"Oh, I went to see your father, today."

"How is he?"

"He wants out of the hospital, but the doctor says he has to stay. Father Vincent was there, too."

"All right. You're doing good, Petey. Stay available."

I hung up without giving him a chance to answer.

There were two things about James Berry that interested me now. One was that he collected art—and Terry Jacks was an artist. The other was that he was gay—and Janet had told me that Terry swung both ways.

Of course, there are a lot of gay men and a lot of art collectors, but this was a possible connection—James Berry and Terry Jacks—and Terry was looking better and better, for taking the statue and for the murder. There was nothing the police could act on, but I had enough to confront good old Terry with.

I called Ed Gorman and asked him what he knew about Tony "Macaroni" Ponzoni's business.

"He broke away from your godfather Barracondi years ago, Nick, and went out on his own. Ostensibly he's in the import business, but Intelligence feels he's using that as a cover for smuggling."

"Of course."

"What?"

"Nothing, Ed. Who's Ponzoni's right-hand man?"

"Fella named DiVolo. He's connected, but talk is he's out for himself, now."

"Did they have a falling out?"

"Not that I know of. Ponzoni's out of the country a lot, and we hear that DiVolo's been making deals on his own. I think he's just trying to get ahead."

"That's an admirable trait in a cheap hood. Who's Ponzoni's main competitor?"

"An operator named Angelo Janetti. He's an out-of-towner who opened up shop here about five years ago."

"Does Mr. Janetti have someone here handling his business?"

"No. He comes to town to handle things himself. He uses the shuttle."

"From where?"

"Boston."

"Boston?"

"That's right. What's the matter with Boston?"

"Nothing, Ed. Nothing at all. Does he have an office here?"

"Warehouse out in Greenpoint. He might have an office there."

"On Franklin Avenue?" I knew I sounded anxious.

"I don't know exactly where. Do you want me to try to find out?"

"No, that's okay."

"Nick, is this the same case you've been working on? If you've got something on Ponzoni or Janetti, maybe you should talk to Intelligence—"

"If I get something on either one of them, Ed, you'll be the first to know."

I hung up, figuring that if Ed had all that information, he must still be in touch with his old office.

I also was thinking about Boston and Greenpoint. Terry Jacks was from Boston, and so was Ponzoni's competitor Angelo Janetti, who had a warehouse in Greenpoint.

Could Terry be working for Janetti? Had Janetti sent him to New York to use Jodi—or her mother—to get into Ponzoni's house? And if so, why was Terry still popping Diane? Could it be that they really had something together? Diane Ponzoni was certainly an attractive woman, but she had to be almost fifteen years older than him.

And what about Carmine DiVolo? If he'd had Jodi held in a warehouse belonging to Janetti, that meant that he'd changed sides—but wouldn't that mean that he and Terry were on the same side? If Terry had the statue, why was DiVolo still looking for it?

I took a pen from the end table and started writing on the backs of the lists I had. I wrote down a bunch of names, again using caps.

PEOPLE CONNECTED TO TERRY JACKS
JODI (definitely)
DIANE PONZONI (definitely)
JAMES BERRY (possibly)
ANGELO JANETTI (possibly)
CARMINE DIVOLO (possibly, if they both work for
    Janetti)

Terry Jacks had to be my man, but why was he still hanging around? Was he looking for a buyer for the piece? If so, had he offered to sell it back to Ponzoni?

My stomach told me it was dinnertime, and I went into the kitchen to feed the furnace. I had some frozen dinners—Hungry-Man style—and put two of them in the oven. I had just done that when Hacker called.

"I've got a name for you."

"Angelo Janetti."

"So, if you already know this shit, why are you bothering me with it?"

"I was just guessing. Anyway, that's what the 'J' stands for. You can tell me what the 'D' stands for."

"DiVolo."

After that he said something else that I didn't hear.

"What? I'm sorry . . ."

"I said do those names mean anything?"

"They mean a lot."

"Yeah, Jodi said they might."

"When did they buy the building?"

"Two months ago."

Hadn't Janet Jackson told me she'd met Terry right after he came to town . . . two months ago?

"Okay, thanks, Hacker."

"Talk to you later."

I hung up and shook my head, which was buzzing. Angelo

238

Janetti and Carmine DiVolo were partners in J&D Imports. That put DiVolo in direct competition with his "boss," Ponzoni. All I needed to do was connect Terry Jacks with Janetti for sure, and I would really be confused. If Terry worked for Janetti, why wasn't he working for DiVolo?

The answer was fairly simple.

Terry Jacks had decided to go into business for himself. Maybe that's why he was still making it with Diane Ponzoni.

A half hour later I had my yellow sheets on the kitchen table, and had gotten fried-chicken grease on the corners from my frozen dinners. I was moving them around when the phone rang again.

It was Cuddy.

"That was fast," I said.

"Surprised me, too. I ran the customary checks—DMV, utilities—and then I called a contact with the police department and had them check for a yellow sheet on Terry Jacks."

"And he had one?"

"A long one, for drugs, both using and peddling. And by the way, Jacks is not his real name."

"What is?"

"He's the son of a big mob guy here in Boston. His name is Janetti, Terry Janetti."

I hung up, but the phone didn't give me time to think about what I'd just learned. I hadn't even taken my hand off the receiver when it rang again. I pulled my hand away as if it had been scalded, then picked it up.

"Mr. Delvecchio?"

"That's right."

I didn't recognize the voice at first, but it wasn't the one that had called me way back when and warned me off.

"This is Anthony Ponzoni . . . Jodi's stepfather?"

"Yes, Mr. Ponzoni. What can I do for you?"

"I'd, uh, I wonder if you'd be able to come out here now."

"To your house?"

"Yes."

"It is rather late, Mr. Ponzoni," I said, and I had a lot to think about, too.

"It's about Jodi."

"Really? Do you know where she is?"

"Well, it's not about Jodi, actually. It's more about the missing sculpture and a boy Jodi knows."

"Mr. Ponzoni, I'm getting confused—"

"Jodi was seeing a boy named Terry Jacks, who lives in Manhattan. I just received a call from that boy."

Uh-oh, I thought, a man answered, and Jacks was too dumb to hang up.

"And?"

"He said that he has my art piece and is willing to sell it back to me."

Bingo.

"I see."

"I'd like you to make the buy for me, Delvecchio."

"You're going to pay?"

"Of course. I have to have that sculpture back."

"Why?"

"Could you come here so we can discuss the details?"

I looked at my watch, which is something I do when I'm thinking. Sometimes I don't even see it, it's just a habit.

"All right, Mr. Ponzoni. I'll be there as soon as I can."

"Good," he said, and hung up.

You're welcome.

240

41

This time I took Jodi's car, not worried about whether Ponzoni saw it or not. I had a feeling we were coming up on come clean time.

I pulled up in front of the house at eleven P.M. and rang the bell.

"I'm glad you could come," Ponzoni said, admitting me. "Let's go into my study." He either didn't notice the car or didn't show that he did.

On the way to the study we passed the living room and the kitchen, and Diane Ponzoni wasn't in either room.

"Is Mrs. Ponzoni asleep?"

"My wife is out," he said, and didn't elaborate. I had visions of her lying in bed next to Terry Jacks when he called her old man and offered to sell the sculpture back to him.

He closed the door to his study and said, "Can I get you a drink?"

"I don't think so," I said. "It's late, and I'd like to get this cleared up."

He regarded me for a moment, then went around behind his desk. It was made of oak, and dwarfed the room, which was rather small but well furnished. Expensive rug, small portable bar, well-crafted bookshelves, everything the successful suburban businessman could want.

"All right, then," he said, lacing his fingers together, "let's get it all cleared up, shall we?"

I sat down and said, "Fine."

"I remember you, Delvecchio."

"Good, I remember you, too."

If he did recollect me, it had come to him after our first meeting. I was sure he hadn't placed me then.

"Actually, I remember your father from the docks. He was a hardnose. Are you a hardnose?"

"It's probably the only thing I inherited from him."

"Good. It's an admirable trait."

"You should know."

"You're right, I should. It got me where I am today."

"Which is where?"

He stared at me for a few seconds and then said, "Fair enough. If you're going to work for me, you should know a little bit about what I do."

"You're in the import-export business."

"Import is a nice way of putting it," he said. "I smuggle."

"What?"

"Anything I can. Drugs, artifacts, precious gems. You name it."

"And what's the story behind this 'hole thing'?"

242

"Hole thing?" he asked, looking puzzled.

"That's what Jodi calls it."

"Oh, I see. Yeah, I guess that's as good a name as any."

"What's in the doughnut, Mr. Ponzoni?"

"Doughnut—oh, the hole thing. Well, I don't think I'll tell you that, Delvecchio—can I call you Nicky?"

"Only if I can call you Tony Macaroni." His jaw tensed at the sound of his old nickname, and I said, "I prefer Nick."

"All right . . . Nick. I'm not going to tell you what's in the thing, because finding out will be added incentive for you to get it back. Am I right? You're curious about what's in it?"

"There is something in it, then?"

"More than you'd think."

"What's that mean?"

"It's not the only thing missing from the house."

"What else is missing?"

"A list, from my desk."

"What kind of list?"

"It's a list of names, new contact points, that I'll use in my business."

"Terry Jacks has that, too?"

"He doesn't know it."

"How's that?"

"The list is in the base. I put it in there before I sent it back here from Mexico."

"You don't have a duplicate?"

He shook his head.

"Can't you get one?"

"It would embarrass me to have to call Mexico and ask for it. I think you can see that."

He was right, I could see that. The people he was working with wouldn't think much of him if they found out that he had . . . misplaced this list so soon after they had given it to him.

"It also wouldn't do you any good if Janetti got that list."

"Janetti?" he said, frowning. "What's that bastard got to do with this?"

Was it possible that he didn't know?

"I assumed you knew that Terry Jacks was Janetti's son."

"What?"

He exploded out of his chair, standing straight up and staring at me as if I had just told him his pecker was on fire.

"His son?"

"Yes."

"That bastard sicced his son on me—on my stepdaughter?"

If you only knew the whole of it, I thought.

"It makes sense," he said. "He used Jodi to get into the house and then grabbed the piece."

"How did he know what piece to take?"

"That's a good question."

"I think I may have the answer."

"What?"

He started to sit, and I stopped him.

"You might jump out of your seat again."

"Why?"

"Carmine DiVolo."

"I knew it!" he said, crashing his fist down on the table. "I knew that prick was up to something."

I told him about the warehouse in Greenpoint, and he just stood there, nodding his head.

"Carmine's a fool. Janetti will use him and throw him away."

"So DiVolo knew what was in the piece, passed it on to Janetti, who passed it on to his son."

"But what's the kid doing offering to sell it back to me?"

"He's gone into business for himself. Trying to get out from under Poppa's thumb."

He sat down, considering that.

244

"I guess you're right. You've done pretty well with all this, haven't you?"

I shrugged.

"I stumbled onto a lot of it. How much does the kid want?"

"A hundred grand."

I whistled.

"Have you got that kind of scratch?"

"I will tomorrow night. That's when he wants it."

"You want me to pick it up and pay him."

"Actually, no . . ." he said, "the kid is the one who asked for you."

That surprised me.

"We've only spoken once."

"If I didn't believe that, I wouldn't have called you. We discussed some go-betweens, and he's the one who brought you up."

"Why doesn't he want you to bring it?"

"My guess is he's afraid of me . . . or maybe he's just real cautious."

"How do you want me to handle this?"

"You'll do it?"

"I'd like to see this through to the end, yeah—but when it's over, we have to talk about Jodi."

"What about her?"

"When it's over."

"All right, fine. I'll get the money together tomorrow afternoon. You be here at eight to pick it up. He's going to call us with the exchange point."

"My guess is it will be either Greenpoint or Manhattan. I'd prefer Manhattan. Greenpoint's too deserted."

"We'll find out tomorrow."

I stood up and said, "Just let me get this straight so I know

245

what I'm doing. You want me to pay him and pick up the piece?"

"I don't expect you to whack him out," Ponzoni said. "I know you wouldn't do that, but if you could get the piece back without paying him . . . well, that'd be worth ten percent of what you save me. Understand?"

"I understand, Mr. Ponzoni." I walked to the door and said, "I'll see you at eight tomorrow."

"Bring your hard nose, Delvecchio," he called out after me. "You might need it."

The fucker picked Greenpoint.

I think I know why.

One, he had a key.

Two, by using his father's warehouse, he was thumbing his nose at his old man.

Kids feel like doing that, sometimes. I know. . . .

I returned to Ponzoni's house that night after lying to a lot of people.

I lied to Jodi, telling her that I had a lot of checking to do that day and couldn't stop in to see her.

I lied to Sam when she caught me going out. I told her I was going to see Jodi, which didn't seem to sit well with her, but if I had told either one of them the truth, they'd have wanted to go with me, for their own reasons.

I lied to Father Vinnie, telling him I couldn't come by to see Pop that night because I had something to do. Well, it wasn't a real lie, just a lie of omission—but maybe when you tell a lie like that to a priest, it's real. I don't know . . . who cared, at that point.

So I told a bunch of lies and showed up at Ponzoni's at eight. Not only did I bring my hard nose, but I brought my snub-nose as well. Actually, my .38 wasn't a snub-nose, but I couldn't resist the pun. . . .

The attaché case was chock full of money, more money than I had ever seen in one place at one time . . . in one lifetime!

Ponzoni let me look at it for a few moments, then slapped the case shut.

The phone rang.

"Yes," Ponzoni said into the receiver. Then "Yes, I have it." He listened again and then replied, "I believe he knows where it is."

I mouthed "Greenpoint," and he nodded.

"Midnight," Ponzoni said, and I grimaced. Greenpoint at midnight was not my favorite place in the world. "All right, he'll be there, just make sure you show up with—hello? Damn it, hello?"

He slammed the receiver down and said, "The little shit."

I agreed wordlessly.

"You heard."

"Yes. Greenpoint, midnight. I assume it's the warehouse?"

"Yes. I have a good mind to call his father . . ."

"Would he believe you?"

A small smile formed on his lips, and he said, "No. We've been business rivals of one sort or another for too long."

"Do you have anything to eat in the house?" I asked. "I haven't had dinner."

He stared at me for a few moments, then understood. It was ten after eight and the meeting wasn't until midnight, and I had no intentions of wandering around with a hundred thousand dollars in an attaché case until then.

"I'll have Diane fix something for both of us."

Asking for something to eat was also my way of finding out if Diane Ponzoni was home or not without actually asking. Obviously, she was, and I hoped to be able to make sure that she stayed home, one way or another.

He started around the desk, and I said, "What about the money?"

"Bring it," he said. "You might as well get used to carrying it now."

I picked it up and didn't know how to react to the weight, since I didn't know what I'd expected. It was neither too heavy nor too light.

He left the room and I followed, carrying a hundred grand of Tony Macaroni's hard-earned money.

42

I took Jodi's car to Greenpoint. I figured I was sacrificing it in a good cause.

The breeze off the East River was cool and damp, but it had nothing to do with the chills I was feeling. I was about to walk into a dark, empty warehouse with a hundred thousand dollars in my hand and a gun on my hip. For some strange reason, my mind was not at rest.

The dockside door of the warehouse was open, as promised, and I stepped inside. My muscles were tense, and I knew that if I was alive tomorrow, my back was going to hurt because of it.

I pulled the door shut behind me and thought about the last thing I had said to Ponzoni as he showed me out the door.

"Do me a favor, Tony."

He'd started a bit at my use of his first name, but then said, "What?"

"Keep your wife home tonight."

"My wife? What do you mean?"

"Let's talk about it when this is over, but in the meantime, try to keep her home. Okay?"

Frowning, he said, "She doesn't have any plans to go out that I know of."

"Good, try and keep it that way."

I'd left him on his doorstep, still frowning. Maybe he'd gone inside and asked her about it, and her affair with young Terry Jacks—né Janetti—was out in the open.

I didn't delude myself about why I was in that warehouse. Sure, there was Ponzoni's promise of ten percent of a hundred grand, but I was there to get the answers to a lot of questions.

I hoped Terry Jacks was in the mood to answer them.

Apparently, young Terry was not intending to keep me waiting so as to make me nervous and testy, because no sooner had I shut the door behind me than the lights went on.

Brightly.

I squinted and raised one hand to shade my eyes, in an attempt both to spot him and to save my eyesight.

"Do you have a gun?"

"Yes."

"Throw it away from you, where I can see it."

I did as he asked, and the gun clattered and slid across the floor.

"Do you have a gun?" I asked.

"Yes, and it's pointed right at you."

"This would be a lot easier if I could see you," I said. My

250

eyes were adjusting to the light, but I still could not locate
him.

"I'm up on a catwalk above you," his disembodied voice
called out. "Is the money in that attaché case?"

"It is."

"Open it."

"How do I know you have——"

There was a shot, a loud one that reverberated through the
empty warehouse—and it was totally empty. Either it was between shipments, or it was simply a dummy.

"Now you know. Open the case."

"I am opening the case." The shot gave me no choice.

I set it down on the floor, flipped the catches, and opened it
so he could see the contents.

"Dump it out on the floor."

I dumped it. It made a nice-looking pile on the floor.

Something struck me on the shoulder lightly, and I jumped
back. It was a canvas sack, sort of like a mailbag, and it was
dangling from the end of a rope.

"Fill it up."

Beyond giving orders, Terry was not being very talkative.
One thing was happening, though. Because of the disembodied
quality of his voice—like a voice on the phone—I was starting
to identify him as the man who had called me that first night
and warned me off.

Question number one had been answered.

I picked the money up off the floor a couple of bundles at a
time and filled the canvas sack.

"Okay," I said when I was done, "it's full."

He started to haul it up, but I held tight to it.

"Where's the sculpture?"

"I have it with me. Let the money go, and I'll give it to
you."

"Send it down—"

"I've got to haul the rope up in order to send it down. I don't have another rope."

I held on to the bag.

"That's the only way it's going to be done, Delvecchio. Let go of the rope!"

Well, there went my ten percent—I only hoped that he would actually send the hole thing down. I mean, why would he keep it?

I released the rope and the bag went straight up. I thought I could see him on the catwalk, but there were shadows toward the ceiling and I couldn't be sure.

"Okay, Delvecchio," he called out, "here comes the hole thing. Enjoy it."

Suddenly something was falling toward me, and I jumped out of the way just in time to avoid it. It struck the floor and broke into dozens—hundreds?—of pieces.

The lights went out at that point, and I was in the dark with my gun somewhere on the floor, and the only part of the sculpture that hadn't been smashed to smithereens was the hole.

I moved quickly after that.

It was easy for me to find the door I had come in by, and I left it open behind me while I went to get Jodi's car, which—surprise, surprise—was still there. I didn't have a flashlight, so I did the next best thing. I drove the car up onto the dock and stopped it with the headlights shining on the doorway. I got out of the car and went into the warehouse, and the headlights gave me enough light to see.

I found my gun, and the attaché case, and the pieces of the statue. I gathered up as many pieces as I could and dropped them into the attaché case. I found out that there was another part that had not been smashed, and that was the base, which was solid and survived the fall with only a couple of chips to show for it. It was fairly heavy, and I put it in the case with the rest of the pieces.

If there had ever been anything hidden in that hole thing, it sure as hell wasn't there when it hit the floor.

I ran out of the warehouse then, got into Jodi's car, gunned it, and headed for Manhattan.

Would Terry Jacks be dumb enough to go back to his apartment?

I was going to find out.

During the ride across the Fifty-ninth Street Bridge something became increasingly evident to me as I passed a car stuck in the right lane.

Terry had not been alone in that warehouse.

He couldn't have been up on the catwalk and at the main light switch at the same time, so he had an accomplice.

I wondered if Tony Macaroni had been able to keep his wife home, after all?

The doorman at Terry Jacks's apartment house was very cooperative—as would most people be, confronted by a twenty-dollar bill.

I was carrying the attaché case with me when I reached his door. Maybe I thought I'd really get the money back, or maybe I just didn't want to take a chance on losing the hole thing now that I had finally found it.

I tried the doorknob right off and found the door unlocked. I started to take my gun out of its holster, then pulled my hand away as if the thing was hot. I didn't want to take it out unless I had to, and I was fervently hoping I wouldn't have to.

I opened the door and stepped into the apartment. It was as it had been the last time I was there, stereo equipment and a lot of easels; otherwise it was empty. If Jacks hadn't come back here, then he was holed up somewhere with his money, and I

253

didn't know how I was going to find him—unless I could find out from Diane Ponzoni . . . and that was only if *she* wasn't gone, as well.

I found the phone and called Tony Macaroni.

"Did you get it?"

"I got it," I said, not bothering to tell him the shape it was in. "Is your wife home?"

"Of course she's home. I don't appreciate these insinuations you're making about my wife, Delvecchio."

"That's tough. Go and check and see if she's home."

He started to protest, then told me to hold on.

When he came back he said, "She's in bed, reading. What's this all about?"

"Later," I said, and hung up.

I put the attaché case down on the floor and opened it. I took out the base and fiddled with it until the very bottom of it slid away and a piece of paper fell to the ground. It was an 8½-by-11-inch piece that had been folded several times, and when I unfolded it, I saw that it was covered with typewritten names and addresses, as well as some numbers I didn't understand. I refolded it and put it in my pocket, then threw the base back into the case and closed it. I picked it up and was about to leave when I remembered Jacks's bedroom. I figured I might as well check and see if he'd left anything behind.

As it turned out, he hadn't left anything behind—*he* had been left behind.

Dead.

43

"Let's go into your study," I said when Ponzoni opened the front door of his house.

"Fine," he said. "We have some things to get settled."

More than you know, I thought.

In his study I asked, "Is your wife still upstairs?"

"Yes, asleep. What's—"

"And she never left?"

"Delvecchio, what the fuck are you trying to say about my wife?"

"Tony, Terry Jacks is dead."

"What? I thought you said you wouldn't—"

"I didn't, but somebody did."

"Suppose you just tell me what happened?"

I did, starting from the point where I entered the warehouse. I altered things very little. For one thing, I told him I had gotten the hole thing back, but I didn't mention its condition. I also told him that I hurried to Jacks's Manhattan apartment to try and get his money back for him.

"What made you think he'd be there?"

"I didn't, but where else could I have looked?"

"Who killed him?"

"If I knew that, I'd know who was in the warehouse with him."

"Wait a minute, wait a minute . . ."

I gave him a moment to gather his thoughts. Go ahead, Tony, I thought, put it together. You're a bright boy.

"Is that why you've been asking about my wife? You thought she was Jacks's accomplice?"

"I don't know about being his accomplice, Tony, but I know she was his mistress."

"His mistress?"

"All right, 'mistress' is a very genteel word for it. They were fucking."

When he swung, I was ready, and he was only half serious, anyway. It was as if he felt obligated to give it a shot, and in his legbreaking days it probably wouldn't have mattered that I was ready. He was much better then. As it was now, I moved aside and the force of his punch threw him off balance, causing him to stagger past me.

"Come on, Tony, cut the crap. I'm not making this up to piss you off. All you've got to do is tell her he's dead and then ask her."

He righted himself, and I waited to see if he was going to throw another punch.

Instead he said, "All right, it makes sense. Janetti sent his son in here to romance my stepdaughter, and somehow the kid

256

decided to do the same with my wife. That makes me a cuckold, and I'll live with it. Did you get the piece?"

"Pieces," I said. I set the attaché case on the desk, opened it, and said, "I got the pieces."

"Jesus," he said, staring at the rubble in the case. "Where's the—"

He stopped and picked up the base.

"Where's the what, Tony?"

"The paper, where's the piece of paper?" That wasn't what he was going to say originally.

He pried the bottom off the base, stared, and then dropped it back into the case.

"Have you got it?" he asked, turning to face me with his hand out.

I thought about holding out on him, but decided against it. I took it out of my pocket and gave it to him.

He took it, went around his desk, sat down, pulled out a checkbook, wrote me a check, and handed it to me. It was for considerably less than ten percent of a hundred grand, but I'm no dummy. I took it, but not without opening my mouth.

"This is all you want from me?"

"You did your job."

"What about your wife?"

"That's between me and her."

"And what about whatever else was in that thing?" I said, pointing to the case.

"Who said there was anything else in it? Did you see anything in it when it shattered?"

"No, it had already been taken out by then."

"What had?"

"Whatever was in it!"

"I'm getting tired of playing charades, Delvecchio. It's time for you to leave."

"What about the hundred grand?"

"For all I know, you killed Jacks and have the money."

"That's crazy."

"Maybe, but the money's gone, and I'm not going to worry about it. It's a business write-off." He stood up and said, "I'll show you to the door."

"You expect me to buy this act? You don't care that your wife cheated on you, helped her lover get a hundred grand out of you—"

"He's dead, isn't he?"

"He is, and I'd like to know who killed him."

"Well, I wouldn't, so when you find out, don't tell me."

In that moment I wondered if maybe Ponzoni hadn't had somebody waiting at Terry's apartment when he returned. Somebody to kill him and relieve him of the money and whatever else he had that belonged to Tony Macaroni.

"I'll find my own way out."

"Do that."

"Oh, one more thing."

"What's that?"

"Jodi."

He waved a hand negligently and said, "Tell the little bitch to come back or stay away, it's her choice."

I went to the front door, folding the check he'd given me and putting it into my pocket.

Money's money, and he was right. I'd earned it.

It was getting light when I left Ponzoni's house.

On the way back to my apartment I tried to figure my next move.

Other than the killer, I knew of two people who knew that Jacks was dead, Ponzoni Macaroni and me. Even if Ponzoni didn't know when I called him, both of us knew that I had been in the apartment—and the doorman had to be added to that list. That meant that I had to make a call to the cops about the

258

body or risk the possibility of losing my license. That was why I had called them and waited for them to arrive at Jacks's apartment.

When the cops arrived, I had given them the bare bones of what I had been doing there—without naming my client—and then invoked the name of Inspector Gorman to get away from them early. It had also taken a promise that I would reveal my client's name (a) only after clearing it with him, or (b) if my license depended on it. There is no legal client confidentiality between a P.I. and his client. That only works for lawyers.

Before leaving Ponzoni's, I decided not to tell him about the cops and my promise to them. My intention had been to tell him to have his lawyer draw me a check so I could claim confidentiality when the time came, but his attitude had changed my mind.

Fuck him.

What was my next move? Finding Jacks's killer? That was the police's job. So was finding James Berry's killer, although they hadn't been doing very well. Jacks might have been good for that, and now they'd probably never know.

All along, my job had been to find the hole thing and fix it so that Jodi didn't have to worry about Stepdaddy getting mad. That was done.

I had also been interested in what was inside the sculpture that made it so valuable, but that was just curiosity. I'd survive without the answer.

By all rights, I was through with the whole episode.

When I got to my apartment, I called Hacker's number and talked first to him, then to Jodi.

"Jesus, Nick, it's seven o'clock in the morning," Hacker groused.

"I know. I've been up all night. Has Jodi been there all night, Hacker?"

"Sure she has. She's still asleep."

259

"The phone didn't wake her?"

"Phones are off except in my room. She couldn't hear it. What's up?"

"I'm about to cut her loose. Put her on."

"Jeez, she's asleep, Nick."

"Wake her up, Hack."

He sighed and said, "Hold on."

I waited while he plugged in one of his other phones, and then Jodi came on the line sounding half asleep.

"Nick, what's wrong?"

"Nothing at all. You can go home now."

"What? Home?"

"Go home or stay away, your choice, little girl, but take my advice."

"What?"

"Get a job and a place of your own. Things are going to be a lot different at home."

"What do you mean?"

"You'll find out. If you want my advice, go home only long enough to collect your things."

"When will I see you—"

"I'll call."

I hung up before she could say anything else.

File this one under closed cases.

I had just about decided to give my brother a call before getting some sleep when somebody started banging on my door. It sounded uncomfortably like Detective Matucci's knock, but the voice that called out with it wasn't Matucci's.

"Nick, come on, open up!"

It was Sam.

I opened the door, and she said, "Where the hell have you been?"

"I've been working all night, Sam, and I just got home. Can this wait?"

"No, it can't—"

"I was just about to call Vinnie and find out how Pop is—"

"Your father's home."

"Home? They let him out of the hospital?"

"Yesterday—"

"Why?"

"If you'd let me tell you," she snapped, putting her hand over my mouth.

"What?"

Her face split into a beautiful, wide smile, and she said, "They've released the hostages. Your sister's coming home!"

44

Two days later Father Vinnie, Pop, and I picked up Maria at Kennedy and brought her home. This time when the neighbors came, I didn't have Vinnie kick them out. In fact, we had a hell of a party, with neighbors, family, and friends.

The house was packed, and we had catered food and a well-stocked bar, and music, and it all drove Maria into the backyard for some privacy.

"Hi," I said, coming up behind her.

She turned and looked at me, and I saw a different Maria than I had ever seen before. There was a haunted look to her eyes. The horrifying experiences that she had been through had changed her, and I had the feeling that my little sister had finally grown up.

"Would you mind giving me a hug?" she asked.

"Hey," I said, opening my arms, "what are brothers for?"

She put her head on my chest and said, "Pop looks bad."

"He'll be okay, now that you're back."

"You all fought, didn't you?"

"Like cats and dogs," I said, "but people react differently in bad situations, kid. That's how we got through it. How did you get through it?"

"Well, after we were released, at our debriefing we were told by an expert that we might need some help readjusting to normal life after the experience we'd been through. This expert even suggested that some of us might need professional help."

"A psychiatrist?"

"Yes, but I don't think I need that, Nicky."

"Why not?"

"Because the whole time I was there, waiting to die, I kept one thought in mind."

"What was that?"

She looked up at me and said, "I knew that if I got out of there alive, I was going to divorce Peter."

I squeezed her and said, "Good for you."

"Shall we go inside and drink to it?"

"Let's go."

I decided I'd never ask her about her affairs, or Numbnuts's affairs, or who had whose first. I didn't care. She was alive, she was back, and she had just taken a huge step toward making her life better.

Later, a huge bouquet of flowers arrived for Maria, who excitedly opened the card. I was hoping they weren't from Numbnuts, trying to make points now that she was home.

They weren't.

263

"Who are they from?" Father Vinnie asked.

She looked at Vinnie and then at me.

"Uncle Dominick."

There was a moment of silence at the mention of the Barracuda's name, and then I said, "Well, put them in some water."

Pop pushed his way to Maria and, putting an arm around her, led her away saying, "Aye, old Dominick was gonna send in a team to get you . . ."

At another point I found myself in close proximity to my father, who was having a ball now that Maria was home.

"Nicky, my boy," he said, putting his right arm around my shoulder. He had a drink in his other hand, and some of it sloshed over onto the floor.

"How you doing, Pop?"

"Great, just great. Isn't it great?"

"It's great, Pop."

I found myself wanting to get away from him. In his present condition he had totally forgotten the harsh words that had passed between us, but I hadn't.

He laughed and said, "We're a family again, huh, Nicky?"

"That's right, Pop. Just one big happy family." I eased out from under his arm and said, "I'd better check and see how the food's holding out."

I left him standing there with his arm out and a puzzled look on his face.

As I left the room, I came face to face with the stern Father Vinnie, who had obviously heard the exchange.

"Nick, come on. You can't hold the things he said against him. Maria's home, and everything is back to normal."

"You're wrong, Vinnie. Nothing's normal, and we're all going to have to deal with that, sooner or later. You'll see."

He shook his head and stepped aside to let me by.

Maybe he'd never see.

264

Once or twice during that welcome-home party, or victory party, or whatever you wanted to call it, I could have sworn that I saw faces of people I didn't know, but I didn't care. *Everybody* was welcome that night.

Well, almost everyone.

I was standing at the food table, having finally decided to have something to eat, when someone came up behind me. I'd started to turn when I felt something hard poke me in the small of the back.

"Just stand easy, Delvecchio."

I didn't know the voice, but I knew that poke in the back.

"What do you want?"

"You and I are leaving this party."

"For how long?"

"Maybe for good."

"I don't know who you are," I said, "but I'm not leaving—"

"You want this welcome-home party to turn into a funeral?" he asked, jabbing the barrel of the gun deeper into my back.

"All right, look, you want to talk, let's talk," I said. "We'll go for a walk."

"No," he said, changing his mind suddenly about taking me away. "We'll go out into the backyard, where we can be alone but where I'll still have access to these nice people with this." He drove the gun hard against my back again to bring his point home.

I was torn between staying at the house and trying to force him to take me somewhere else. While we were close to the house, there was a chance that someone else could get hurt, but if I let him take me away from the crowd, there was a good chance I could end up dead.

"Okay," I said, "the backyard."

I turned away from the table, which had been set up in the dining room, led the man through my father's room—which

265

had been made off limits during the party—and into the back-yard. With a gun in your back a thirty- or forty-foot walk can be like thirty or forty miles, and all the way I was trying to figure out who this dude was.

I could only come up with one answer.

When we got to the backyard, he said, "You can turn around now."

I turned to face a tall, dark-haired, rather oily-looking man who was holding a gun in his right hand.

"Carmine DiVolo, I presume?"

"Good guess."

"I don't remember inviting you to this bash."

"I saw on the news that your sister was one of the released hostages, and I figured you might be having some kind of a full house. If it was my sister, I would."

"I'm touched."

He made sure I knew he still had the gun in his hand by pointing it at me.

"Why don't you hold that a little higher so everyone can see it? That's just what this party needs, a bunch of cops."

He frowned, then lowered the gun to waist level, keeping it more or less pointed my way.

"Okay, tell me what you want so I can go back to the party."

"What I want is what was in that sculpture."

"What?"

To be honest, ever since I had heard the news about the release of the hostages, I hadn't thought much about Jodi Hayworth or the sculpture. I hadn't even heard from Jodi and didn't know if she had taken my advice or not, but then I'd been out of my apartment more than in.

"That piece of sculpture you bought back from the kid for Ponzoni."

"What about it?"

"I want what was in it!"

266

"I don't even know what was in it, let alone have it."

"You got it from the kid."

"I got a million pieces from Terry Jacks, DiVolo. There was nothing in that piece of crap when he dropped it from the catwalk in that warehouse." Then it hit me. "Wait a minute. You must have been there. You must be the one who hit the lights."

"I was there, and we were supposed to meet at his apartment to divvy up the money except my goddamned car died on the Fifty-ninth Street Bridge."

I remembered the car I had passed on the bridge that night, stuck in the right lane.

"Jeez, if I had known that was you, I would have stopped and picked you up."

"I didn't need you to pick me up. I got to Terry's building just as you were leaving . . . after you killed him and took the money and what was in that sculpture."

"He was dead when I got there, DiVolo. How do I know you didn't kill him?"

"I didn't—wait a minute. Let's don't turn this around."

"I think that's what's happened, DiVolo. Things have gotten turned around—on you."

"What do you mean?"

"Well, let's see if we can figure this out. You and Jacks conceived this plan to rip off Ponzoni."

"No, no, that was Janetti's idea. He sent the kid here to romance Ponzoni's wife's kid, Jodi, and to get his hands on what was in that sculpture."

"How did you come into it, then? I thought you worked for Ponzoni."

"I did, but the kid offered me a lot of money to help him show his dad something, and I agreed. I was getting ready to split from Ponzoni anyway, so I figured I might as well do it for a hundred grand."

"A hundred grand? Terry was going to give you the entire hundred grand?"

"That was the deal, but now you've got the money, which is what I wanted, and you've got the . . . whatever was in that statue thing, which is what the kid wanted."

"Wait a minute, let me get this straight," I said. "*You* don't even know what was in it?"

"He never told me."

"DiVolo, believe me, I don't have your money, and when Terry Jacks, or Janetti, dropped that statue on me, it broke into a million pieces. There was nothing in it."

"I know that," DiVolo said irritably. "Terry took it out before he dropped the thing on you, but you—or somebody—killed him and took it out of his apartment."

Well, that was a load off my mind, anyway. By saying that me or "somebody" had killed Terry, he was saying that maybe he was starting to believe that I hadn't done it.

"Look, DiVolo, put the gun away and come inside and have something to eat. I think we've both been taken in this thing. I delivered a hundred grand for a worthless statue, and you've been cheated out of the same hundred grand."

He studied me for a few moments, then said, "Ah, shit!" and put the gun away. "I believe you."

"Then come inside and eat."

"Nah, I've got to find out who took my money—besides, I already ate. Can I get out of here without going through the house?"

"There's a gate over on this side."

DiVolo nodded.

"Uh, look, sorry to interrupt your party. I'm glad your sister's okay."

This was crazy. We were parting like a couple of buddies, me inviting him inside, and him telling me how happy he was for me.

"Good luck," I said, because I couldn't think of anything else, and he just nodded and started around the side of the house.

"Hey, Delvecchio," he called from out of the darkness on the side of the house.

"Yeah?"

"Watch out for the old man."

"Yeah, sure . . ."

As I started back for the house, I suddenly realized that maybe he hadn't been talking about my old man, but Terry Jacks's father.

Was he warning me to watch out for Angelo Janetti?

After the party we decided that Maria would spend the night at Pop's and then in the morning would go with Father Vinnie to her house to collect her things. Both Maria and Vinnie wanted to keep me away from Peter, just in case he was there. As much as Vinnie didn't like him, he certainly wouldn't get into a fight with him. Needless to say, Numbnuts hadn't been invited to the party, and he'd had the good sense not to try and crash it.

Sam, on the other hand, had been invited. I had come with her to the party, and we drove back home together in her car. Apparently, any differences we'd had over the past week or so had faded away in the light of Maria's return.

"Your father looked very happy tonight."

"He was drunk."

"Maybe he had a right to get drunk."

"Maybe."

She was driving, keeping her eyes on the road ahead, and I stared out the passenger window. I was thinking about Jodi's hole thing again, since the subject had forced its way back into my mind at gunpoint.

269

"Nick, you're not going to let what passed between you and your father affect your relationship, are you?"

"My relationship? I don't even know what kind of relationship I have with my father."

"Some things were said under the worst of conditions—"

"Let's just forget about it, Sam."

"None of my business, huh?"

"Mmm."

"What's on your mind tonight, Nick? As the night went on, you got quieter and quieter."

"Murder."

"What?"

"Murder is on my mind."

"What murder?"

"Actually, it's two murders."

"What two murders?"

I started talking, then, telling her about James Berry, about Terry Jacks, and about Jodi's "hole thing." It was the first time I had laid the entire thing out for her—or anyone.

"A McGuffin."

"Not now, I'm not hungry."

"No, not a McMuffin, silly," she said, "a McGuffin. Don't you know what a McGuffin is?"

"No."

"Alfred Hitchcock coined the phrase. It's what everyone in his movies is looking for."

"What is?"

"The McGuffin."

"But what is it?"

"That's the beauty of it. It doesn't matter what it is, it's a McGuffin."

"And that's what this sculpture was?"

"Right."

"That's real helpful, Sam."

270

"What are you going to do?"

"The problem is I shouldn't do anything. It's up to the cops to catch the killers."

"But you feel a responsibility to find the murderers?"

"No, Sam, that's in your books. I'm just curious."

"About what in particular?"

"Well, Berry doesn't bother me so much. I'm pretty sure Terry killed him, but who killed Terry and took the money and the . . . McGuffin, well, that bothers me."

"So find out."

"That'd be like working for nothing, though, and that also only happens in your books."

"You wouldn't be working for nothing if you found that hundred thousand dollars."

She had a point there. Oh, not that I'd keep the entire amount, but maybe Ponzoni's offer of ten percent would still be available.

"Well, then, all I've got to do is figure out who killed Terry Jacks."

"Wouldn't it have to be someone who was in on it from the beginning?"

"Sure."

"Somebody who knew all of the principals involved?"

"Uh, sure. Well, at least somebody who could have introduced . . . Jodi and Terry . . ."

"Do you know anyone who fits that bill?"

After a moment I said, "You know, I think I do."

EPILOGUE

I waited for her outside of where she worked and then followed her home.

It was no easy task, waiting on that street, trying to look inconspicuous. I finally settled for a table at a sidewalk cafe down the block, from where I was still able to see the front steps of the store.

Finally she came out, and I stood up and followed her.

I had spent the day wondering if this was the right thing to do or not. Of course, Sam said it was, but that was because it made me fit into the mold of her fictional heroes, Marlowe and Archer and the rest.

I finally decided to do it because if I didn't, the curiosity would eat at me for a very long time, wondering if she had done it.

When she turned into Horatio Street, I knew she was going straight home, and I was glad. I would have hated to have to tail her around the city as she hit all of her favorite watering holes, or whatever. This way I could brace her in her apartment, where she just might have everything hidden—if she was the amateur I thought she was. I was willing to give her the benefit of the doubt on that count.

After she used her key to enter the building, I hotfooted it up the front steps and managed to catch the door before it eased closed. I allowed it to close, but just didn't let it close enough to lock. Through the dirty glass I could see her walking down a long corridor and then up a flight of stairs. She never once looked back.

I checked the mailboxes and saw that her apartment was on the second floor. I opened the door and started quietly down the hall. I had reached the foot of the steps when I heard a door close from upstairs. I went up the steps quickly, found her door and knocked. I didn't want her to be able to catch her breath.

When she opened the door, the surprise on her face was obvious.

"Oh, hi."

"Remember me?"

"Sure, you're Jodi's detective. Still working on her case?"

"More or less. Mind if I come in?"

"No, not at all," she said, swinging the door open. "Come on in."

I entered and found myself in a small kitchen. There was one other room beside the bathroom, and it held a bed, a couch, a T.V., and some stereo equipment.

She closed the door, and I turned to face her. She was still very sexy, with her cornrows and her bodysuit—different color

273

this time, but same effect. Still very attractive, even if I did think she was a killer.

"Tell me about it, Janet."

"About what?'

"About killing Terry and taking the hundred thousand dollars out of his apartment."

"I don't know—"

"The thing I really want to know is how you got past the doorman without him seeing you. The rest I can figure out for myself."

Actually, that part wasn't really important. The fire escape to Terry's apartment was one possibility. However she did it, my whole case began with the assumption that she had, one way or another.

She folded her arms beneath her very fine, very firm breasts and said, "So go figure."

"I think Terry came to town and met you and got you to meet Jodi and then introduce her to him. If I ask Jodi, I'll bet I find out that she met you after Terry hit town."

"I've already admitted I introduced them. So what?"

"So I think you did more. I think when Terry got the idea to cross his father, he got you to go along with it. Who else did he know in town? DiVolo? Carmine was just a stooge, hardly the kind of guy that Angelo Janetti's son would want to partner up with. You, on the other hand, were dynamite in bed and real sharp, weren't you? A hundred grand would take you a long way."

"Don't you wish you could find out how good I am in bed, white boy?"

I ignored the remark.

"You introduced him to Jodi, and through Jodi he met her mother. Why did he ever start an affair with her, I wonder?"

"He dug her." The look on her face plainly said that she couldn't understand it. "No, really, he was into older women.

He said he liked to fuck somebody's mother every once in a while."

"How did you feel about that?"

She shrugged.

"I didn't care."

"But you were there when he wanted you, weren't you? And when he needed somebody to hook him into Jodi Hayworth? He used DiVolo for the scut work—like grabbing Jodi, trying to scare me off, and going to the warehouse with him—but he probably wanted to save you for the real important stuff, like holding the money for him?"

"You're telling it."

"You got into his apartment, and you were waiting for him to come back from the warehouse with the money. I think when you saw it, you decided that instead of playing house you deserved an even split. All that money got to you, didn't it, Janet? You asked him for half, and maybe he laughed, maybe he said that you were along for the ride for as long as he wanted you, and that's all. How close am I?"

"So he dumped me," she said, shrugging again. "I been dumped before. That don't mean I shot him."

"What?"

"I said that don't mean I—" She stopped short as if she had just realized that she was the first person to bring up the fact that he had been shot. The papers had said that Terry Jacks— also known as Janetti—had been killed, but the cops had deliberately left out the manner in which he had been killed. They wanted to sit on that for a while, at least until the phony confessions had stopped coming in. They had found drugs in Terry's apartment, and some sexual paraphernalia that indicated that Terry went both ways, and when sex and drugs were involved, the weirdos came out of the woodwork and started confessing to everything.

"How'd you know he had been shot?" I asked, feeling like I

was in a bad T.V. show. Rockford or Harry O., entrapping the killer through the slip of a tongue.

Hey, sometimes it happens that way in real life, too.

She was smart enough to know, however, that she didn't have to admit anything. After all, there was only her and me there. Unlike Rockford or Harry Orwell, I had not thought to bring along a police friend to stand just outside the door and listen for the confession.

"You're still telling it."

"I'm almost done. From the beginning, then. I think that Terry had DiVolo find out from a helpless old man in a hockshop who had bought the statue after Jodi hocked it. Terry found out that the buyer was a homosexual and used that to get into the man's house. I think he killed him and stole the statue. I think he took whatever was in the statue out and then offered to sell the statue back to Jodi's stepfather. He probably wanted to make Jodi part of that deal, but she got away. He tried locating her, then went ahead with the sale, anyway, suggesting that I act as middleman. The sale went down, except I got stiffed, and then when he tried to stiff you, you shot him. The gun was probably his own, which you found in the apartment and used. Come on, Janet, I'm running out of breath. It's time for you to help me out here. Tell me it was an accident and that you didn't plan to rip him off and kill him all along."

"You been watching too much T.V., Jim. This here girl ain't saying nothing to nobody that she don't have to. You can't prove a thing!"

She was cool, too cool to be the amateur I had originally thought she was. She was a barracuda, and had probably had an eye on ripping Terry off the whole time. He was trying to prove to his father what a top operator he was, and he got taken off by a sweet, young, black barracuda.

"You're right about that," I said, "I can't prove a thing, but there is something I can do."

"What's that?"

I stepped past her and opened the door.

"First I can plant a bug in Tony Ponzoni's ear about where his money is."

"You would—"

"And second, I'm sure Angelo Janetti would like to know who killed his son."

"You can't do that—"

"It's up to you, babe. Turn yourself in by tomorrow, or buy a plane ticket to take you a long way from here. You won't get away, but you might last a few months. These men play dirty pool like you've never seen played uptown."

I left her standing there with her fists clenched. Somewhere in her apartment was a hundred thousand dollars and what Sam called a "McGuffin." Sam was right about one thing. It really didn't matter what the McGuffin was.

I walked across the Brooklyn Bridge, once again experiencing that relieved sensation of coming home to Brooklyn.

My curiosity about who killed Terry and took the money was assuaged. The lady had not protested enough, and had been just too cool about everything. I was satisfied that I had constructed the sequence of events from Jodi's hocking of the hole thing to Terry Jacks's death in the proper order. I'd check with Gorman tomorrow to see if she had turned herself in. If she had, I'd find out just how right or wrong I was. If she hadn't, I'd have to see if I really wanted to throw her to Ponzoni and Janetti or tell the cops what I knew. I'd also have to give them DiVolo's name as the man I thought killed the old man in the hockshop, and Terry Jacks's for killing James Berry.

Then again, I could just forget it and let DiVolo and Janet Jackson get away with murder.

My choice.

Sam was going to love it. She'd say it was the way these kinds of books are supposed to end.